WHAT READERS ARE SAYING:

"One powerful piece of writing."

"Creepy as hell."

"Couldn't stop reading."

"Shocking."

"Psychologically complex."

"Hot and terrifying."

COMING SOON:

Open Endings

In marriage, trust is everything.

2017

Based on a Screenplay by Scott Frazelle

AN EROTIC THRILLER

S.L. HANNAH

CONCEPT
PUBLISHING

the adventures of hannah
CONCEPT PUBLISHING

Published in the United States by The Adventures of Hannah–Concept Publishing. www.theadventuresofhannah.com

Paperback ISBN 978-0-9768869-5-2
eBook ISBN 978-0-9768869-6-9

Printed in the United States of America

Editor: Jennifer Thomas
Associate Editor: Scott Frazelle
Developmental Consult: Mallory Braus
Text Design: The Adventures of Hannah
Cover Design: Joshua Jadon

First Paperback Edition

For Scott—
Your unconditional love, support, and dedication
make my world go 'round. We did it.

The Need

An Erotic Thriller

ONE

I've been watching her for a while now.

She's mesmerizing. Totally comfortable in her skin. I can tell by the way her bra strap falls down her shoulder and strands of sweaty hair matt to her face. She doesn't care.

The wall behind the bar and bottles of booze is all mirrors. The deep thump of the bass reverberates in my chest, and the air, moist with sweat, envelopes me like an unwelcome fever. I continue to watch her dance in one of the reflections as stringent liquor coats my palette distastefully. I don't want to be obvious.

Her taut frame is sandwiched between an attractive couple. They don't look much older than me, but they look fashionable and carefree, like they belong in a place like this. She's suggestively pushing back and forth to the DJ's evocative beats, letting her blonde mane bathe in the crest of the girl's neck, until the guy grabs it and pulls it back, like he doesn't want to get left out of anything. Their hands wander freely. It's almost as if they're not on a dance floor, but in a bedroom. Doing it standing up. She pulls the girl in tightly. She's commanding. How I wish I was.

I turn my gaze back to my near-empty drink and the cell phone next to it. Still no response from my boyfriend to my voicemail and several text messages and it's almost midnight. *Where is he?* I swirl the ice cubes in my glass.

He knows I'm not really into nightclubs. The drinking, the posturing…it makes Erik feel like he's part of a squad. It makes *me* feel like I don't fit in. But I don't want to disappoint him, or myself. I can't spend all of college immersed in books. These are supposed to be the defining years of my life, brimming with experiences that you reference forever, experiences that help you figure out who you really are.

I look back up at the mirrored wall. She has this look on her face, like there's nowhere else she'd rather be. As if time has stopped just for her, so that she can feel every tensed, slick muscle, hear every throb of desire. *Will I ever feel that?*

That's why I agreed to meet him here. In this beat-up industrial warehouse amidst the architectural mishmash of buildings that make up downtown L.A. Having grown up on the West Side, I've only ventured to this part of town once or twice, and never at night, but I wanted to be open-minded, or at least play the part. I get so tired of the image everyone has of me. Smart, moderate, cautious, agreeable. A straight arrow. Or maybe that's just the image I've created for myself because it's…easier.

I take a last sip of my margarita and push it towards the bartender. He asks if I want another. I shake my head. I've already waited for Erik longer than I should have. I toss my cell phone back in my purse and turn to leave.

"Leaving so soon?"

I nearly bump into the woman I've been watching all night.

She's taller than I thought, and glistening. She's intimidating now that she's looking at me the way I've been looking at her. Examining every response and inflection.

"I was…uh, waiting for someone." I fidget with the strap of my purse. "But I think he got caught—"

"Well, I'm *someone*," she interrupts, tossing her hair out of her face. "Heather." She holds out her hand.

"Angie," I respond, shaking her hand and noticing her firm grip.

"Can I buy you a drink, Angie?" she asks without letting go.

A flurry of habitual thoughts run through my head. *I've already had a drink, I don't even like to drink, I'm tired, I didn't dress right, I have to get up early to study.* And, *what would Erik think?*

And yet…

Before I have a chance to decline, she finally releases my hand and calls out to the bartender. She tells him to get me another and her a beer. He seems a lot more eager to tend to her than he was to me.

A couple minutes later, he places fresh drinks in front of us. She doesn't seem to be concerned about paying for them and neither does the bartender.

I pull out my phone and glance for any messages.

"Maybe you should check his Facebook page," she says, like she's already determined my situation. "It's made it so much easier to learn everything you want about a person's life."

"I deleted my Facebook page last year."

She pushes my cocktail towards me. "You want me to check for you?"

"No." The icy wet tumbler stiffens my fingers. "And you'd have to be friends with him anyway."

She slowly nods and then wraps her lips around the tip of her beer bottle before taking a long swig. "You like to watch?"

The question makes my cheeks burn. I look away from her and taste my margarita. It's stronger than the last one. So strong it makes my brow crinkle.

She twirls her bottle slowly on the bar. "I think people who watch have really great gut instincts."

I smirk. Being the child of two scholars has made me an emphatic logical thinker. Growing up, every question was met with a step-by-step program for how to research the answer…when all I wanted was a conversation. "Why do you think that?"

"Because they witness enough mistakes."

I attempt to down more of my potent cocktail, uncomfortable with how quickly she's presuming. "Well, I don't think that going with my gut is going to work too well as a molecular biologist."

She shoots me an inquisitive look, so I explain to her that's what I'm studying at UCLA.

She tells me she also went to UCLA and at once I'm more at ease. She tells me about her quest to study photography and how she eventually had to drop out because she couldn't afford to continue taking classes.

"You probably don't have to worry about that," she says pausing mid-sip. "Do you?"

The glass sweats between my fingers. "My parents are faculty. I don't have much choice when it comes to my education."

"It's not always a privilege, is it?"

I shake my head and smile sheepishly. "They decided I should take the summer semester. While they travel. Again."

Her face crinkles as if it's the most unreasonable thing she's ever heard.

"They call it work because it's with a bunch of other archeologists in their department, but—"

"It's just an excuse to wife swap."

I nearly spit up my margarita, giggling at her assertion.

Her manicured fingers stroke the neck of the bottle. "What do your friends think?"

I usually hate telling people that I don't really have any. It makes me out to be so lame, when in reality I just haven't met a kindred spirit in a long time. But I don't go there. I tell her that most of the people I go to school with are either way too into their studies...or way too into themselves.

She clinks her glass to mine, and we continue bonding over campus life and how ludicrous it can be. We decide the workload and expectations make it hard to have any fun, and that there are no guarantees anyway that you'll end up with your dream job. We talk about the "chosen ones," with their rich parents who always seem to donate just enough at just the right time, and the ones who have no business being there except to fill a quota. And by the time we finish talking about the various school rivalries, our drinks are gone.

"You want another?" Her shoulder brushes against mine.

I feel a little dizzy from the two I've already had. "I don't know...I should probably go home."

She places her hand on top of mine and I feel that firm grip again. "What's your gut telling you?"

An anxious sensation runs down my spine.

TWO

I'm sitting on her worn brown leather couch. It's in the middle of the huge loft she lives in, which was a further cab ride than I expected. There's an old trunk in front of the couch, which she uses as a coffee table. A lock hangs from the hardware. *Does a key hang somewhere else?*

Behind the couch is this bed. It's completely daunting. It looks larger than a California King, with bedposts made of thick steel and a mass of dark-hued sheets and pillows and blankets heaped on top—like they haven't been folded since they were bought, but have been used plenty.

Windows line an entire wall of the space, but they only allow in a sliver of moonlight and a view of an equally long brick wall. No wonder the place is so quiet. Not what you'd expect from a part of Los Angeles situated between two major highways. It's hard to tell whether she even has any neighbors. All you can hear are the swirling blades of the lone fan mounted to the ceiling struggling to move the thick air.

"Do you believe in love?" she asks as she finishes rolling a joint. And then, before I can answer, "Do you wanna get high?"

She senses my hesitation and towers over me, even more now than she did at the bar. Her blonde hair is still a mess. Like that bed. A few flimsy clasps barely hold her black sparkly shirt together, and her tan leather skirt is so short I can see right up, especially with the way she's sitting.

I wave off the crinkled roll and turn my gaze away, but not before she notices. Her lips turn up into a slight smile before she leans over and grabs a lighter sitting on the dusty trunk. I can see the start of her black lace bra.

"I'm not sure what to think of love," I tell her as I adjust my jean skirt, not wanting to expose anything I don't want her to see.

Her eyes dance in amusement.

"I mean, my boyfriend and I are in love," I correct, wanting to sound more assured.

The day Erik approached me in the coffee shop, asking for my help with some trig assignment, that was definitely love—or at least love at first sight—for me.

I felt giddy and sick all at the same time. I'd never talked to someone like *him* before. He was all actor-good-looks and muscular frame. My pencil literally dropped from my hand when he later told me during our study session that "smart and pretty is a lethal combination."

I'm suddenly conscious of the fat roll pinching against the button of my jean skirt. I know I've put on five pounds since he and I first met. The stress from school and my parents makes me binge eat sometimes. I straighten up like I did in all those interviews at the other schools I applied to, trying to impress important strangers with an image of a self-assured go-getter. Interviews that my mother said were pointless. Both my parents lived and breathed UCLA and couldn't understand why I wouldn't want to do the same.

I tug at a thin strand of hair near my chin. "Do you think I should do something different with my hair?" I know it's a stupid question, but everything about the way her hair masses around her face and her clothes drape around her frame seems so stylish.

She moves in this particular way that makes her rib cage jut out to one side and a clasp of her top slides open. She watches me watch her as she casually reaches for the bra strap that keeps sliding down her shoulder and pulls it back into place.

"You think that will make him love you more?" She places the joint between her lips.

I shrug, wishing I hadn't brought it up, then notice that her lips look dry. Like they need to be licked and moistened.

As if sensing my observation, her tongue circles her mouth carefully, so as not to miss a spot. "You need to believe in yourself more, Angie." She lights up the joint. "We all know who we really are on the inside. Most of us just spend our lives fighting it, trying to make everybody else happy. The right person will make you feel like you don't have to change a thing."

"Erik's not like that." I look towards my purse, wondering if I've embarrassed myself enough yet. I should check my phone for messages once more and figure out how to get home. The tips of my fingers reach as far as the trunk and then press into the hard, wooden boundary instead.

My parents are the ones who always make me second-guess, particularly my mom. She's always badgering me about what I should look like to attract the kind of guy she thinks I should be dating, or how I shouldn't be dating at all until I get my doctorate in molecular biology—sex is too distracting. But I don't want to turn this into a therapy session.

A waft of cool air slips through a few of the opened windows and momentarily cools the sweat at my hairline. I'm not quite sure what I want this to turn into…

Heather holds out the joint to me and I politely decline again. She chuckles, but not in a pitying kind of way. In the kind of way that makes me feel at ease around her. Like I'm hanging out with an experienced fraternity sister who's slowly going to help me unravel the secrets of the world.

"It's a hot night tonight, isn't it?" She leans back, and this time slides open the few remaining clasps of her top so that it falls open.

I nod, staring at the lace of her black bra. The saliva is thick at the back of my throat. I gulp and can't help but compare her breasts to mine. Hers are smaller, and positioned higher on her rib cage. They look firm, not floppy.

Erik loves the way mine jiggle, of course. He's never shy about grabbing them or sticking his erection between them, like they're some kind of masturbation prop. I'm all right with that, I guess. As long as the lights are off.

"I'm getting this place for a steal." She exhales another hit and slides her legs the opposite way, the black of her underwear peeking through again. "They won't put in an AC unit."

My tongue runs forcefully across the ridges of my teeth, trying to keep it together.

I turn my focus away from her, to all the portraits hanging on the walls. Each is a series of women. Some dressed, some nude, but all with a similar look on their faces, like they're in the midst of rapture. "You're a good photographer," I tell her.

Her fingers lightly graze my thigh. "Thank you."

She positions herself closer, like a man positions himself when he's getting ready to make a move on you.

Everything around me feels like an electromagnetic force. A fundamental interaction in nature that's unstoppable. My heart races and my head feels dizzy from an evening of built-up curiosity. Not about what it would be like to be with a woman, but about what it would be like to be with *this* woman, or just *be* this woman.

"Do you ever show them anywhere?" I need to keep the conversation going somehow, even though I can tell it's probably not going to stall her for long.

She slowly climbs up the couch, crowding me…

"No." Her mouth sweeps my neck. "I just use them for inspiration."

Hot lips press against mine. The skin around them is soft. Not like the stubble Erik lets grow all the time. And instead of a sterile drugstore-brand aftershave, I smell her musky perfume mixed with the pot on her breath. My insides melt.

Her lips start to nip at my lips. They're thin, not puffy like mine. Erik calls them blowjob lips. He can be such a jock sometimes. I bet Heather would never say something like that.

I allow her tongue to slip in. It invades immediately, like a search-and-rescue mission. A pressure builds between my thighs.

I suddenly find I want more than her lips to touch me, and that I want to touch her. But I'm not sure how. Is it like touching a man? Is it like touching yourself? I lean back a little, to slow things down, but she pulls my legs up on the couch and leans between them.

"You're so refreshing," she says as her hand goes up my loose black tank top. I worry about the way my boobs always fall heavily to the side and about that horrible beige thing I have to wear to keep everything in place. *Will it make her want to stop?* But she moves so slowly and deliberately, carefully inching around me, that I quickly forget everything I've taught myself to be critical about and instead become unbearably aroused.

She tugs on my nipple underneath my bra. Gently at first, then harder, until my lower back is slick. My kneecaps are clenched so tightly, they could crack a Brazil nut, and a pool of liquid has formed in my underwear.

I boldly place my hand on her bra. She puts her hand over mine and guides it inside the tight binds of that lace, until I'm cupping her breast. My breath hastens as I feel the rubbery outlines of a nipple that isn't familiar, and she smiles. Like she's just won a big stuffed prize at the fair.

She guides my hand out from inside her bra to the back of it, helping me unclasp the strap. It falls off, and her thick nipple hovers over my face until its texture is against my mouth. I slowly take it in, feeling the supple skin with my tongue, and suck on it like a lollipop. It gets bigger. A lot bigger.

She lets out a moan and grabs the outside of my thigh, pulling me closer. Her grasp moves up my leg until I feel her pull the elastic of my underwear to one side. It makes me flinch. I let go of her nipple.

"This is going to feel really good, Angie," she says, nuzzling against my skin to comfort me. "We need each other right now."

I know she's right, even though I don't have the courage to say anything.

Her fingers wander through my pubic hair, until they're at that slippery spot. I sigh, in anticipation and consent.

One of her fingers begins to circle my labia and another one goes inside of me. I bear down into the sensation, wanting more, and she continues giving me what she knows I need.

My mouth reaches for hers, and this time it's my tongue that firmly explores, as my hips rock up and down. Not because I think that's what they're *supposed* to do, like all those other times, but because I can't make them stop.

Something builds inside of me. Something that I'm only used to experiencing by myself, late at night when I envision the perfect lover. A lover who knows how to please my body without a hint of instruction. A lover who's soft when I want to be intimate and hard when I want…something else.

More fingers swim in and out. The pressure grows. I should stop her. Tell her that what we're doing goes against so many of my guiding principles. But no, I want that release even more. I need the release or it will make me crazy. I start making sounds, stifled cries in between pants. I want more of her. I am barely conscious of wildly kneading her skin between my fingers.

I can't stop my thunderous climax if I tried.

For a few moments we just lie there, as if the world has stopped and forgiven everything once considered a sin.

She releases my hands and kisses me again, but this time more swiftly. Methodically, her clothes are pulled back into place and the blanket that's bunched up on an arm of the couch is casually thrown over me. I watch the shadow of her form walk away from my heap of exhausted bones and emotions. *Did I do something wrong?*

I think about following her or at least calling out her name, but my limbs feel too heavy to even drag and my mouth is too parched. I quiet my mind, reassuring myself that tomorrow, when I'm back in my own bed, this will all read differently. I clasp the edge of the thin cotton blanket, bury my face in it, and pass out.

THREE

I wake up even more dehydrated, head pounding. Light casts through that wall of windows. I adjust my bra and tug on my top. I unhinge my underwear from the crack in my behind and pull my skirt down. I look around for my purse and phone, until my gaze falls on the woman from last night. She's sleeping.

Quietly, I creep over to that huge bed she's on and take a better look.

She's pretty. In that way women are who are older, maybe nearing forty, but still look young. They eat healthy, or eat very little, or substitute booze for food, and work out a lot, even if that just means three nights a week on the dance floor. But their skin looks a little more fragile. And their creases are multiplied in more places. And if they let their hair dye go a few weeks too many...but still, you hope you'll look as good as they do when you get there.

I notice how nicely tanned her shoulder is and how strong her arm looks. I look up the bedposts. Large rings and shackles dangle around them. *What does she use those for?*

I'm embarrassed.

Memories of what happened last night flood back, making me want to slip out before she wakes. I never thought I'd have a one-night stand—and with a woman. My feet shuffle quietly on the floor as I pick up everything I think I came here with and tiptoe to the door I remember coming through last night.

The exit is confusing. There's a deadbolt, but no handle. I press a hand against the cold steel and try to slide the door first to one side and then the other, to no avail. *Damn it.*

I spot a two-by-four leaning against a cabinet next to the door. *Is that what I have to use to get out?*

"You in a hurry?" Her voice echoes across the expansive room.

"I…well, kinda need to get going…" I sheepishly turn around, knowing I sound like a kid.

She's propped up on one elbow, still wearing that nice black lace bra.

I feel my face redden, thinking about how I touched it last night. "I'm supposed to meet my—"

"Boyfriend?" She cuts me off and reaches for a shirt. "Well, it would mean a lot to me if you stayed for a bit." She throws on a plaid button-up and pivots around. Her lean long legs dangle, nearly reaching the floor. "We could…talk."

She slides off and starts walking towards what must be the kitchen, even though it's no more than a fridge shoved between tall shelves, a plywood countertop, and a big butcher block for a table with two adjoining stools. "You *do* drink coffee, don't you?"

I try not to stare at the way she saunters, her matching black lace underwear peeking out from under the edge of the frayed shirt.

I'm stunned by proportions that look even more perfect in the daylight. My behind is so much bigger than hers. Erik likes to tease me about my "Black bootie." Thinking about him makes me reach into my bag for my cell phone. Still no response from him to my text messages or voicemail.

Something's not right. Erik has never stood me up before. Sure, he *just* graduated while I decided to take summer classes, so things have been a bit off, but… We're just going to have to make adjustments to our schedule. It doesn't necessarily mean we're drifting apart.

I'm probably overreacting. We've never spent every waking moment together or kept tabs, and we *have* only been dating for five months. Maybe I just don't get relationships. He *is* my first serious boyfriend. Or as serious a boyfriend as I've had. Before Erik, there were a couple of friends who were boys. Sometimes we'd have sex, though it was never very good. This is probably just a normal misunderstanding. Maybe our first big fight. I shouldn't be so paranoid.

I loosen my grip on the phone.

"A watched pot never boils." I'm snapped out of my internal rumination by a line I remember her saying to me at the bar last night, too.

I put my phone back into my bag and walk over to where she's standing. I try to get comfortable on one of the metal stools as I watch her microwave two cups of water.

I think back again to last night. The bar, and how loud it was, the dance floor, and how crowded it was, and the drinks she kept buying me while I waited for Erik to show up or at least call. *Was she hitting on me all night?* I don't know. I rarely know when someone's hitting on me.

I do know she allowed me to vent and feel angry and disappointed without feeling sorry for me. That felt good. *And after the bar?* I'm sure after a few days, I'll look back on this experience with appreciation. I rarely let loose, and I never feel daring enough to…experiment. *Live life with reckless abandon.* That's the sticker I once saw on this girl's notebook in my organic chemistry class. I could probably confide to someone like her about what I'd done and she'd understand.

Heather opens the door of one of the tall shelves and takes out a plastic container, then scoops out some dark brown powder into each cup. She opens her fridge and takes out another plastic container and pours a little of something into each cup.

I want to tell her that I don't take cream, only sugar, but she seems so certain in everything she does, I don't want to interfere.

"Bet this wasn't in your plans for the weekend," she says, placing both mugs on the thick wooden block that separates us.

I focus on the creamy contents. "No, it was a lot different."

"Different is good though. Right?"

Different was actually one of the best nights of my life, but I can't tell her that. I'm certain the admission would come with some sort of expectation that I can't possibly fulfill. I run my hand over the handle of the mug and realize her skin felt just as smooth. I slowly lift it and take a sip. It's way too sweet, but I decide it's alright.

My phone starts to ring from inside my purse and I reach for it.

She stops my hand. "Still hoping to hear from your boyfriend?"

The way she says it makes me feel bad. I try to pull my hand away, but she grips me harder. Like she did last night.

"I know you want to believe you and Erik are in love because it makes things easier. Doesn't it? It's easy to believe that when you go back to his place, he'll apologize and you'll have sex with him. And that will be enough."

She loosens her grip on my hand.

I decide to reach for my mug instead of my phone.

"And he'll fuck you good all weekend. Even make breakfast for you, which is out of character for him. So you'll forgive him, drink beer in the afternoon with him, watch TV until his dick gets hard again. And then you'll go back to your life on Monday and wait for him to call you about next weekend…and then you'll wait for him to propose, and then you'll wait for him to tell you he wants to make babies with you, waiting, hoping…that it will all somehow be enough. That his needs will somehow fulfill yours."

I take another sip of her sweet concoction, hurt by her change in tone. "He's not a bad guy. And last night…" I feel defensive. "Last night you got me drunk."

She throws her head back theatrically and bursts out in laughter. "I got *you* drunk?" Her laugh grows louder and more exaggerated. "I suppose you also think I forced you to grind all over me on the dance floor and then dragged you to my place, and that when we got acquainted and intimate…it wasn't really you."

She pauses and looks away. "You think I'm just like some guy? That I like to prey on women and lure them back to my place and take advantage of them? And hope they sneak out in the morning before we have to talk?" When she looks back she has tears in her eyes.

"I'm sorry," I say. "I didn't mean to imply that. It's just, I've never done anything like this before. Not even with a guy. I'm not familiar with one-night-stand etiquette. What do you want me to do?"

Her look eases and she wipes each eye. Her hand trembles as she caresses my cheek. "You're so young, and so pretty."

The comment, coming from someone like her, is such a compliment. I've always considered myself rather plain.

"Why don't you stay here? With me." She chews on a nail, before catching herself and pulling back her manicured hand. "I mean, for the weekend," she adds, as if I would presume something else.

The proposition startles me. I can only imagine what spending the weekend with her would be like. She knows her way around my body so well...it sends tingles to my most private of parts. I *do* want to experience more of that, especially more sober. But I feel awful for betraying my relationship with Erik, regardless of what happened last night.

Maybe it wouldn't have to be sexual. Maybe we could bond as just friends, and if she wanted more, I'd be clear about how important my relationship with Erik is to me right now. Although I can't imagine that a woman like her wants to be anything but sexual.

She holds out her hand. "Come with me. I want you to see something."

I slowly take her hand. We walk to the center of the room and stop in front of that oversized bed. She steps closer to me. Her nearness sends electricity down my spine. I wish I didn't find her so attractive.

She brushes a strand of hair off my face and smirks, as if sensing my mixed emotions. Then she lets go of my hand and lifts an electrical cord from the floor. It's attached to a small control box.

She walks the control box over to a camera affixed to a tripod. I remember noticing it last night. I fidget with my fingers, not knowing what to expect, and eventually slide them into the pockets of my jean skirt.

A flash goes off and I realize she's just taken a picture of me. This makes me want to fidget more. I really don't like having my picture taken. It makes me compare myself to others. I never look as good as they do. My hair always looks flat. My skin is never even. The bags under my eyes make me look older. My nose sticks out too much. And if I'm not holding my head high, I have this awful double-chin that makes me look overweight...

"Relax," she says, snapping another picture of me. But I can't. "Am I going to have to get you drunk?" she teases. I try to smile, but looking down at the wedges that have rubbed blisters into my pinky toes, I'm wishing I hadn't stayed for coffee.

She puts a hand on her hip. "Maybe this will help." She presses a button on her control box and the sunlight fades under the whine of an electric motor. Industrial shutters close over the tremendous wall of windows. Senses heighten in the near dark, I hear more clicking as globes of diffused light come to life and the low hum of music in surround sound.

"You can be free here." Her voice is further away now amidst more camera clicks and flashes. "Free to do whatever you want and be whoever you want."

It's easy for someone who looks as good as she does in black lacy underwear to talk like that. She doesn't understand that girls like me always have limits, and always will. "I don't know how to be free," I blurt out, frustrated. I cover my face with my hands to shut out the camera and the lights.

The clicking stops. In fact, the room falls silent, except for the slow techno-beat thumping in my eardrums. When I lower my hands from my face, she's standing close to me, swaying her hips and undulating her body, like she did at the bar last night. I watch her, illuminated by the various lights, looking warm and vibrant and alive in a way that makes me jealous.

She places one hand on my hip, the other still holding her camera. She pulls me close, the way she did on the dance floor, except right now I feel stiff.

Her lips brush against my ear. "Scream," she tells me.

"What?" I scoff, feeling ridiculous.

"I know that's not what you call a scream," she says, grabbing a fistful of my hair and yanking it back—hard.

It feels like she's just ripped a clump of roots from my scalp. I let out a high-pitched wail.

Flashes from her camera go off near my face.

She pulls my hair again, this time using it to lead me over to the tripod.

She replaces the camera and forces me to look at the viewing panel.

I watch images of myself move across the small screen.

"You see how beautiful you are?"

What I see is a girl who looks better when she's being forced to scream than when she's trying to be normal. "You take great pictures," I tell her, like I did last night.

She smiles, finally letting go of my hair. "Stay put. You might feel more free *behind* the camera."

She disappears into the darkness, away from the lights. I smooth out my hair. My hand is shaking.

Moments later, she holds out the mug I was drinking from earlier. "In case you need something to calm your nerves," she says, dropping her plaid shirt and walking to the bed.

She hops on and starts to vamp. Messing her hair, playing with her bra straps, spreading her thighs apart then back together, moving her behind to the drumbeat pounding through the air.

I take a long gulp of the liquid in my mug, now much cooler and sweeter.

Composing myself with a deep breath, I press a button at the top of the camera. It snaps a picture.

The flash sets her on fire. She starts rolling her head, reaching for a bedpost and grinding on it like a stripper pole, then dropping into the sheets, running her hands all over her body, lingering at her private parts.

I continue snapping pictures, playing with the zoom, in and out, as she watches me watch her through a lens that both magnifies and distorts all our most intimate flaws.

She jumps off the bed and struts towards me. Skin moist, mouth slightly parted, eyes dark and hungry.

My body heaves in anticipation.

She takes the coffee mug out of my hand and places it on a shelf behind me, her gaze never leaving mine. I feel a knot forming in my gut.

She takes my hand away from the photo capture button and leans in, ready to lead me astray again…

My body feels on fire, but I've already decided that I can't. Last night, I convinced myself that Erik was a terrible boyfriend, maybe even with somebody else, and deserved to be punished. But I know he's not. I shift my head to the side.

She takes my chin and redirects me.

I pull away. "I don't—"

"You don't what?"

I tell her that I don't want to be seduced by her again because it makes me uncomfortable and confused about Erik…and it was never my intention…and I'm sorry to have sent any mixed signals.

She drops her hand and with the same coolness she used to peck me on the cheek last night, picks up the control box.

Within moments, the mood lighting is off, the shutters are whirling up, and the only sound is the real world blasting fiercely through the windows.

My hands feel clammy and sweat beads my brow. "I'm sorry."

She looks at me, vicious. "No. *I'm* sorry. I've wasted my time."

She drops the control box to the floor. It makes a loud, startling clang. I'm nauseous. And not just from her unpredictable nature.

I watch her pick up the frayed plaid shirt she dropped earlier and then open the top drawer of an end table and take out a chain with a key on it.

She walks to the front door, unlocks the deadbolt, and slides it open.

I grab my purse and hold it tightly against my chest, avoiding her icy stare as I walk towards the opened door.

When I step out, the door starts to close immediately.

I turn around and put my hand on the edge to stop her. "I'm glad to have met you." I mean this, even though I don't know exactly what it is she expected from me or that I wanted from her.

She looks away and continues sliding the door.

It shuts loudly.

I get down two flights of stairs and have to stop to wipe the perspiration from my forehead. My heart races like I've been climbing a mountain instead of going down a few stairs. I decide it's this situation that has made me sick, or maybe the alcohol from last night. Yes, it must be a combination of all that.

Down another flight of stairs and I have to sit. I feel weak, like I won't make it much further. I need to call Erik. Maybe he can pick me up. And then I realize that I don't know where I am, well, maybe he can help me figure that out. Or maybe I can map it on my phone. My hand feels like lead as I reach into my bag.

I grasp for my cell phone.

I reach into the side pockets of my purse.

No cell phone.

My head is hot and my body throbs all over. The smell of rat poison makes me dry heave a few times. I pat my face to make myself more alert, trying not to panic.

I just need to go back up there to get my phone. Maybe she can even call me a cab. I can rest until the cab comes.

Slowly I lift myself. The stairs swim in front of me as I climb them one by one, each step feeling taller than the last. I slip a few times and start to crawl, gripping each stair as best as I can.

The air is thick. *Did I eat some bad food last night?* Maybe it was the chicken from the shady taco stand next door to the club.

It feels like it's taken me an hour to get back to her front door. The door.

I lean against it, resting my hot head against the cool steel, and then I knock.

No answer.

I knock again, and again, harder and harder. I scream out her name, banging on that metal divider, even though it feels like I'm going to pass out.

Finally, the door slides open.

She stands with my cell phone in her hand. "Is this all you came back for?"

I can barely catch my breath. I stumble backwards and feel her firm grip on my arm. I tell her I have to lie down. I reach for my phone...collapsing.

FOUR

She keeps repeating her name. *Heather, Heather, Heather.*

As if I'm ever going to forget. Or maybe I will. I'm so out of my mind right now. Like Alice going down the rabbit hole, chasing after a mystical creature, not knowing whether it's good or evil, but unable to turn around. This must be what it's like to be on drugs.

I've never been on drugs.

Or maybe she keeps repeating her name because I keep repeating his. *Erik, Erik, Erik.*

I can see him. I swear I can. He's sitting on the edge of the bed next to me, slouched over like he's pondering his next great water polo move. I've seen him do it before. Strike the air and twist his torso like he's in the water.

He's naked. He's always more comfortable naked and he thinks I should be, too. That's what he likes to say whenever I reach for something to throw over myself after we have sex. Except he's beautiful naked. When he runs his hands through that thick mop of hair, those biceps bulge, those firm abs flex, and those perfectly sculpted thighs ripple…

He turns to me and asks how he can bring me pleasure.

This makes me giggle. He's never asked me that before. I tell him I want him to tie me up. I can't believe those words just came out of my mouth. Like I dug them up from some yearning obscured by years of trying to conform to something else.

He's surprised too. He didn't expect that from a conservative girl raised to get her PhD in something complicated, but then he starts slowly undressing me. He's never done that before either. He's more of a tear-as-you-go kind of guy.

He carefully lifts the tank top off me, and then slips his hands to my back. His big palms press into my skin and his agile fingers unclasp my bra and drag the straps along my arm in an agonizing way. I can smell the zesty soap on his collarbone.

My nipples are already pert. They want attention, but as soon as it looks like they might get some, he teases them instead by turning his head the other way, rubbing them lightly with that stubble of his.

Finally his lips purse around one and he sucks ever more fervently, like he's nursing. It's almost unbearable, but my back arches to get closer.

I ask him why he's never taken the time like this before. He tells me I scare him, and it seems like he wants to tell me more, but rolls me over instead, unzipping the skirt that always fits too tight.

He lifts my ass a little and gives it a gentle smack. I tell him to do it harder. He obliges my demand over and over until my cheeks sting. I like feeling completely under his command. Like he could do anything he wanted right now and I wouldn't want to have a choice in the matter.

He pulls the edges of my underwear lower, until they're all the way down. I feel his tongue at my labia. It runs up one side then down the other and up the middle, and repeats this pattern until everything has become intensely plump. It's pulsing and wet, wanting terribly to clamp onto something that looks impossible to engulf.

I ask him why he rarely services me orally. He tells me he's afraid of disappointing me and then rolls me over again, lifting my hands above my head and anchoring them with some kind of soft restraint. Our hurried breaths sound loud in an otherwise perfectly still room.

He parts my thighs. First the left, then the right, and thoughtfully massages the muscles down to my calves. I'm completely exposed and vulnerable, and it doesn't bother me that the lights are on.

He hovers over me, dragging his thick, hard unit up and down my belly and then pressing it against that place where it could almost go in, but doesn't. I want to grind against him like a wanton schoolgirl, like I've always wanted to, but have never felt comfortable enough to.

I ask him where he was last night. He tells me his poker game ran late. That some woman showed up and distracted everyone and then took them for all their money.

I'm surprised. Poker night is a strictly male-bonding ritual. *Who was the woman?* I ask him this.

He tells me no one really knew her. A leggy blonde in a tight black dress who knew how to stack her cards right. I feel him slowly push inside me, taking away all my jealous notions.

As my hips rise to meet his, I ask him why he didn't at least text to let me know he was alright.

The hard bones of his pelvis dig into mine, creating a distinct pressure against my sensitive nub. It makes me want to wear it down.

His phone died, is what he tells me. And by the time his ride was ready to take him to the club, he was already passed out on a friend's couch.

A wave of rhythm swells between us.

He tells me he misses me. He tells me he's sorry for everything that happened last night. He didn't mean to do it. He didn't mean to stand me up.

She keeps repeating my name. *Angie, Angie, Angie.*

"Angie, it's me, Heather." It's what I hear her say.

And I want to come, but I want to continue the conversation with Erik more.

FIVE

My cell phone is ringing.

I recognize the high-pitched tone that sounds like a steam engine and try to open my eyes, but they're so heavy. I know I need to get it, but I'm so awfully weak. Someone needs to get it for me. I don't want to miss the call. I'm sure it's Erik.

"Hello!" I call out, but my voice is hoarse. "Heather!" I call out again, but it hurts my throat too much, so I stop.

I try to move my arms, but I can't. Something is holding them back, no up, above my head. I try to move my legs, close them together, but I can't. I must still be dreaming, but this time, instead of being in a safe place with my boyfriend, I'm in some kind of danger and unable to run.

The ringing stops.

I pull again. This time harder, until my wrists and ankles start to burn.

I open my eyes. Dim light floods the room.

I'm not dreaming. I'm on her bed. A thin sheet covers me and I can tell I'm not wearing anything underneath. I look up. My arms and my wrists are tied with a thick, braided rope to each of those rings around her bedposts. I look down my legs, and see my ankles have suffered the same fate.

None of this makes sense. *Why would she tie me to her bed like this when I was so sick last night?*

I pull again. Maybe the sweat of my skin will loosen the binds. Perspiration forms around my hairline, and eventually one of the ropes starts to drag over a thumb. My muscles strain and my teeth grit in a desperate attempt to free myself. Finally a hand pops free.

I examine it. It's bloodied and raw, but enough endorphins are running through my body that I barely register any pain. My mind races with thoughts of how to get my other limbs out, until—

Something heavy lands on me. Knocks the wind right out of me and grabs my free hand.

"No, no," she coos, smothering me with her weight, pulling my hand back to the rope. "Hold. Still." She cinches the rope around my wrist—tighter this time. It sears into my skin.

"Let me go!" I cry out, feeling the strain on my throat. I jerk my body, trying to get her off me, the sheet once covering me now a jumbled mess, leaving me naked under her.

"I don't think so," she says, sitting up. Straddling me, she reaches for something and then holds my cell phone close to my face. "Miss a call?" Her hands scroll over the display. "From somebody named Erik?" She clenches her thighs around my ribs. "Is this the boyfriend, the one worth waiting for?"

The heat in the room and her weight around me are making it hard to breathe. "Let me go, please. I…I won't tell anyone—"

She throws the phone to the side and leans closer. "Won't tell anyone what?"

I can smell the chalky powder she's brushed over her skin when her cheek presses against mine.

"That you like to get drunk, and go home with strangers… women…even though you have a boyfriend?" she sneers.

I turn away from her, disgusted by her insinuation because that's not what last night was about. Sure, I wanted to experiment, and hurt Erik a little in the process, but I wouldn't have done it with just anyone.

She twists my jaw so that I have to face her. "Maybe you're confused about what you really want."

My heart pounds loudly in my chest and the sheet beneath me is drenched. "So what if I am!" If all she wants is for me to admit my insecurities about some of my crudest desires, then so be it.

She lets go of her grip around my rib cage.

I gasp for air and am momentarily blinded by the flash that goes off. I shut my eyes tightly, hoping this will all be over soon, until… another flash, and another, and another. "What are you doing?"

Another flash.

"Stop it!" I scream, my voice cracking.

"It's not that simple, Angie."

Another flash.

"You decided to face your demons," she continues, sliding down, hips rocking over mine. "Came up here and did dirty, dirty things, and now look at you." She jerks hard on one of the ropes and my foot flexes. "You know they're not gonna let you walk away so easily."

Tears well in my eyes. Another flash goes off.

She bends down, and I can feel those dry lips at my ear as one of her hands gingerly makes its way down my body. It's soothing in a way I don't want it to be.

Her hand reaches my sex and her fingers circle. I want to press away, but my thighs begin to clench instead. *Why does she have this effect on me?*

"You could be in a lot of trouble, couldn't you?" Her fingers play at my opening as I try to squirm away. "Nobody's coming for you." The tip of a finger pulses in and out. "Because no one knows you're here."

My head is hot. I want her to stop, but I can't seem to say anything.

"That's right. You like that, don't you?" she whispers. Her voice has a hypnotic effect on me.

I can tell I'm getting wetter and wetter down there. My body is responding uncontrollably to her touch, even though my mind is telling me to fight her off.

"And you like being a slut," I finally blurt out.

She stops. Pulls her fingers away and slowly sits up. The camera drops to the bed. "That's how you feel?"

I nod, as tears spill down my cheeks from confusion and relief.

"That's how you really feel?"

"I may not have everything figured out yet, but I know you're taking advantage of me. And tying me up—"

"That's what you said you wanted last night," she cuts me off angrily. "Don't play innocent now."

My mind is cloudy, unable to make sense of it all.

"You're the one who could get in a lot of trouble for this." I yank on the binds. "I want to go home." Her expression remains cold. "Please let me go home," I say more urgently.

She throws her head back, laughing, and then reaches for

something behind her. "I want you to know, I admire you." She starts playing with what looks like a large flashlight until she lifts it and it catches a beam of light. It crackles and a flash of blue emits from two prongs.

Oh my god.

"I admire you for being so…brave." She makes the object crackle again.

I'm frozen with fear, unable to comprehend why she's taking this so far.

"You ever seen one of these up close?" She brings the stun gun to my eye level. "They're amazing. Twenty thousand volts in a single burst, sustainable for up to three seconds at a time."

I take a deep, uneasy breath. "He…Heather."

She pulses the stun gun again, briefly, and then touches one of the electrodes with her fingertip. "All through these two little metal points." She glides her fingers over the device the way she was gliding them over my sex moments ago. "I've heard that it feels like a muscle tear, a hard punch, and snakebite, all rolled into one."

A white flash from her camera goes off in my face.

"When applied correctly, the victim will pull away involuntarily. It's as if the body can sense the potential for more pain and does whatever it can to escape." Another flash goes off. "If it can."

A black-and-white negative of what's in front of me pulses in my head as she runs her weapon across my neck. "Heather, please, don't do this."

"They say that an unfortunately placed hit, say, too close to the heart, or prolonged exposure, could cause death."

The two metal prods are at my chest and another flash from her camera goes off. This isn't the same woman from two nights ago. Every muscle in my body tenses as I try to think of something to negotiate with. "My parents have money," I say with resolve.

Slowly, the tip of her index finger releases from the shutter. Her eyes appear from behind the viewfinder, and the intimidating scepter doesn't feel nearly as depressed into my flesh.

"They're not rich, but they have clout," I continue articulating, confident that I've struck some kind of chord. Her empathy is gone, but maybe her desire for something more tangible isn't. "They... they could arrange for you to finish your degree in photography, or anything else. They could make your life more comfortable."

The edges of her properly plucked brows begin to gather and her lips pucker. "You think I've kidnapped you? For ransom?" She says this as if I've completely misunderstood her motives. "I'm a businesswoman, not desperate, but thanks for the offer." Another camera flash goes off and the negative image throbs madly in front of me as she digs the stun gun deeper.

More tears well in my eyes. "Okay, fine then, you're right. I'm not innocent. I *wanted* to go home with you last night. I saw you on the dance floor, beautiful and carefree and strong, and I thought if I went home with you, I could glean some of that and experience something new." I'm being completely honest because I have nothing else left. "I guess I used you, but I didn't want to hurt you."

The stun gun stops moving around my torso like the Grim Reaper.

"And you...you're right about my boyfriend. I *don't* know if he loves me or is even right for me. You...you're right, you're right, pl...please...you're right," I stammer.

Finally her eyes soften and she rolls over, lifting the stun gun off me. She tosses it and it lands near my face.

I breathe a sigh of relief.

She props herself up with one hand and her other hand begins to glide. "Such delicate white skin." She reaches my stomach and makes circles around my belly button. "Such a beautiful girl."

The look on her face is tender now as she grabs the camera again and starts taking more pictures. This time I don't protest. I look right at the camera and let her capture whatever image she needs. I look over at the stun gun, wishing it to roll away further.

"Except something just occurred to me."

I look back to her.

"You called me a slut."

Before I have time to respond, apologize, or take back everything forthright I've said to her, she pounds the stun gun into my stomach and pulls the trigger.

The intense electricity shoots through my body and my ears ring from a deep internal scream I can't seem to evoke. I feel myself lifting away from my body. Looking down at a girl, bound, naked, and convulsing.

A set of white flashes go off and then I feel her hand stroke my cheek.

"It's me, Heather." Her hand moves across my face. "Focus on breathing, Angie. Don't try to talk, we're not done yet."

Another electric shock rips through my body. I strain upwards and then recoil. The ropes dig harshly, breaking my flesh.

More flashes go off as I spit and choke from trying to suck in air that feels sparse. More clicks and camera flashes, as my eyes roll towards the back of my head.

"Stay with me, baby." I can barely hear her voice. "It's me, Heather, and you're doing so well." I feel her hand press against my face and neck before succumbing to darkness.

"Angie, this is Heather." Her voice is ethereal.

When I'm able to open my eyes I see her beautiful mess of blonde hair framing those big dark-blue eyes, and that long neck leading to the black lace of her bra. She looks angelic. How I want to remember her. How I want her to be.

"Try to get some sleep now, baby," she murmurs.

SIX

Her name was Janelle.

She was this bouncy little troublemaker—at least that's what my mom would say—who joined our class in third grade.

The boys made fun of her because she was half a foot taller and two years older than everybody else, and the girls didn't know how to talk to her because they thought she was dumb, but she didn't seem to mind. She was always happy, and she quickly became best friends with the short, fat girl whom no one wanted to talk to either.

Janelle always had a game she wanted to play, and if she could have gotten away with playing all day, she would have. More than once, her antics got her sent to the principal's office. Sitting in class, reading, writing, even eating was boring she'd say, and by the time we got to fifth grade she'd developed a penchant for risk-taking.

It started out innocently enough. Jumping off swings after

pumping our legs back and forth a hundred times to get to the highest peak, sneaking away during lunch to get ice cream at the gelato bar eight blocks away...but when she once suggested we play chicken crossing the I-10, I knew she was looking for something I couldn't comprehend. I remember wishing I had her resilience and poise, but cowering and watching her instead. Heart thumping so fast the entire time from fear that she would die, leaving me to fend for myself, again, but she made it. And I was in awe of her even more.

By sixth grade, we were in one of those portable buildings. The ones outside of the main school with the bad temperature control. The AC would never work right in the summer, and the classroom would get really hot. Then in the winter, the heater would just churn and churn until our hair stood up from all the static in the air.

Outside our portable was this old wooden crate with a latch. Maybe at one time it held gym equipment, but during our brief tenure it sat empty.

One lunch hour, Janelle decided it would be fun to take turns locking ourselves into the crate to see who could last the longest. Before you felt like the oxygen was about to run out or got so scared you almost peed your pants, although I was sure Janelle never would.

That became part of this new game. Trying to scare one another with stories of ghosts and large poisonous insects, even cold-blooded killers living under the crate with secret doors that only they could open and snatch you up at any moment. But as soon as you screamed "Bubblegum!" it was over. Whoever was on the outside had to undo the jump rope and let you out.

Bubblegum.

That was the word we used to let the other person know we'd had enough of being scared. Bubblegum.

I never lasted long. I was easily terrified. Always had been. I wouldn't even go to sleep with all the lights off in my bedroom.

I hated dark places, so just the anticipation of that heavy wooden lid closing with a thud and the eerie darkness that followed with just a few splinters of light peaking through the dilapidated wooden slats was usually enough for me to scream out "Bubblegum."

One blustery lunch hour following quite a bit of rain, Janelle told me she had a better idea. We would go into the crate together. She would help me stay in there longer. She would help me conquer my fears.

I wasn't sure I wanted to or cared. I would have much rather we stopped playing the game all together. But Janelle always had this insistence. I could rarely deny her requests.

She opened the crate and took my hand. We placed one foot after another inside and barely fit into the cramped space. The hatch came down again and even though this time it wasn't tied shut, I immediately felt my breathing hasten, just like all the other times.

The inside always smelled putrid, like old newspapers and wet animals, and it was exacerbated this time by the humidity in the air.

Janelle grasped my arms with her hands and began chanting words that were indecipherable. I asked her what she was saying, and she said it was a spell to summon the spirits. She wanted to create a passageway between our world and theirs.

I wanted to be strong, but the notion petrified me.

I closed my eyes fiercely and screamed when the wind began to howl between the slats, begging Janelle to stop. She continued her litany and dug her fingers so deeply into my skin that eventually my arms felt numb and all I could hear was our panting breaths and the rain that had started up again outside.

No spirit had come.

Janelle released her grip and let out a howl. She pulled my trembling body close to hers, reminding me of how I had nothing to be afraid of. I barely registered her words and instead focused on the gentle drumming of her fingers up and down my arm, until my nerves began to calm and I felt brave enough to open my eyes.

Open your eyes, Angie.

My corneas twitch to the beat of my own request, trying to lift the lids over top like ill-equipped muscles. But I don't want to be conscious yet. I don't want to deal with the burgeoning situation. I want to revel, for just a little longer, in a happier place.

Do something to get out of this mess, Angie. Open your eyes!

I see a flicker of red light under the edge of a pillow next to me. I clamp my teeth down on the cotton covering it and swing my head.

It's my cell phone.

My hand stretches, but the phone is still inches away.

I pull on the rope. My hand starts to shake and my breath becomes erratic as I crane with unparalleled determination. The rope cuts through fresh scabs and new layers of skin until finally I reach my phone.

I grasp onto it like a life preserver. The red light signals that it's low on battery, as I look around the room and listen for any indication that Heather might be around.

There's no sign of her. My fingers press the three numbers that make most sense: 9-1-1.

I hear the ringing on the other end and pray no one else can. And then: *CALL FAILED.*

No, no, no.

Palms sweating, I dial 9-1-1 again. It rings, and then: *CALL FAILED.*

I pound my head against the mattress. *Why isn't this working?* I can't afford to have the battery die before I reach someone who can help me. I decide to compose a text message instead.

Fingers trembling, I press sequential letters on the keypad: *HELP TRAPPED IN DANGER.* I press the SEND button.

The text message sends. My heartbeat bounces between my ears, and my eyes fixate on the screen as the battery continues to dwindle…until: *NEW TEXT MESSAGE.*

An exhale of relief escapes my lungs.

I open the text message: *ERROR MESSAGE ##7532-911 NUMBER IS A LANDLINE AND UNABLE TO RECEIVE OR REPLY TO TEXT MESSAGES. IF THIS IS AN EMERGENCY, HANG UP AND CALL 911 OR LOCAL AUTHORITIES.*

No! That's not possible.

My mind analyzes who else to call.

I should call Erik. *What if he doesn't pick up the phone?*

My parents are out of the country for the whole summer again. Another journey to another corner of the earth nobody has heard of, except for the other archeologists in their department.

I don't have any close friends whom I feel comfortable enough to involve in something as crazy as this. Janelle is long gone…

I open my short call list and press Erik's name.

He tried to call me. She told me he tried. I'm sure he's worried about me, regardless of what happened last night. Of course he's going to pick up the phone.

I grip the purple silicone protector covering my lifeline, the battery indicator signaling it's almost dead. *Hang on, hang on.* I press the call button.

CALL FAILED.

I carefully type a text to him: *HELP ME CALL ME SOS.*

I hit the send button and close my eyes. For the first time in my life, I pray to a God I've never been taught to believe in.

I look back at the phone.

It starts to power down. I press whatever button I can to keep it alive, but it's no use, the screen goes black.

My devastation turns to anger.

I begin scolding myself. *I never go to bars alone. I barely ever make eye contact with people I don't know. How could I have been so wrong about her? How could one curious night at the bar possibly mean I might die, or become some sexual slave to a psychopath?*

I imagine myself as another statistic. An awful headline in the newspapers. *UCLA Honors Student Missing, Presumed Dead.* The speculation will devastate my parents. *Daughter of upstanding citizens and esteemed scholars found on the wrong side of town.* Perhaps she'd started hanging out with a bad crowd. She was dating a jock, after all, instead of focusing on her studies. So much potential, such good grades, and yet she wasn't strong enough to stay the course.

Sticky flecks of dirt rub off the silicone as my thumb continues to fondle an edge of my phone.

Maybe I was *never* strong enough. At least not on my own. Maybe that's why I spent as much time as possible with Janelle. Before school, when I rushed to meet her at the intersection where she always bought a Slurpee, after school to eat potato chips and dip and cheesecake and all those other things my mom would never let me eat at our house, and on the weekends for sleepovers.

Sleepovers were my favorite. I slept over at Janelle's house as much as possible. It wasn't hard. My parents were always busy and her parents were always inclined to host. They were warm and caring, and they had all these suggestions for things to do...it felt like being with a real family.

It was during one such sleepover that Janelle suggested we watch *Poltergeist*. Classic horror movies were her favorite, she'd told me on several occasions, and watching it with her would be good for me. Another way for me to see how silly it was to be afraid of anything.

I didn't immediately object and wasn't instantly horrified. It'd been a few years and so many more awakenings since the incident in the crate that I started believing I could conquer anything as long as Janelle was by my side. That night, she suggested we zipper our sleeping bags together to be a greater force against anything that might spook us. This is how she explained the strategy and I didn't mind. I liked being close to Janelle. Her frame alone was like a shield, and I huddled close.

Soon enough, though, I was perspiring through my clothes, wishing I could crawl into hers. It was the movie, but also something else. I couldn't stop my mind from wandering into the unimaginable, my ears from hearing suspicious calls, my eyes from seeing disconcerting shadows lurking... I held onto Janelle tighter, telling her to turn off the movie and turn on the lights. Instead, I felt that slow drum of her fingers up and down my arms.

She whispered that she would always protect me...and then she kissed me. The new sensation amidst my fear created a strange aphrodisiac that caught me by surprise. But I never once felt an inclination to fight it—or her—off. I could taste the determination in her mouth and it made me desire what was happening even more. Our hands wandered carelessly over shoulders, collarbones, backs…long after the movie ended. I fell asleep in her arms that night, feeling like I had very much fallen in love.

I look up at the cold frame of the bed, helpless and more scared and alone than when Janelle's parents moved to Sacramento after tenth grade.

Janelle would have never gotten herself into a situation like this one. And if she had, she'd be clever enough to know how to get out.

Unsure of what to do next, I allow my head to rest in the crease of the pillow and my limbs to give into the bonds.

SEVEN

For a brief moment, I imagine I'm in my bed. Cocooned in the canary yellow sheets I bought when I moved out my sophomore year of college. About to drag myself out and feel the fluffy sheep rug my parents brought me back from New Zealand at my feet. Wonder why all my footwear doesn't feel this good.

I'll brush my teeth and look in the mirror, like I do every day. Play with my hair, and that pimple—because puberty seems to never end for me. Then the daunting task of what to wear.

Nothing in my closet fits quite right, or maybe it would on a different body type. I'll settle for the comfortable stuff I always end up wearing and hope it's the day I have my Plant Differentiation and Development class so that I can get into an intellectual debate with Professor Singh about something interesting, like the pathology of cellulose.

Not.

I do have one dress. I call it the Jessica Rabbit dress. It's all curves and cleavage and no trace of cellulite. The black velvet three-quarter-length number I picked out for Erik's graduation just last month.

He was floored. I even got my hair and makeup done for the occasion. We barely made it out of his room on time. I imagined it was what our wedding day would feel like.

"Finally up?" Her voice beckons me back to a different reality.

I watch her move around. Dressed smart in a sleeveless blouse and a pencil skirt, like she's going to an office—not like she's got someone tied to her bed. She goes into her makeshift kitchen, busies about, and then walks over to me.

A coffee mug and first-aid kit are placed on the end table next to the bed before she lifts the lone sheet covering me.

"Don't!" I snap at her.

"There, there," she says like a caring mother, pressing her hand to my forehead. "Shhh…" She strokes back my hair.

"Why are you doing this to me?" I look down at my uncovered skin and see my belly and chest covered in red marks and blisters.

No answer. Instead, she opens the first-aid kit methodically, like a pro. *Does she even realize the kind of hurt she's inflicted?*

She pulls out a jar and opens it, dabs a couple of fingers inside, and then smears some white goo on one of my red marks.

It soothes immediately.

"You have to let me go," I implore, watching her hand deftly attend to each of my wounds and slowly rub in the cool ointment. "Are you listening to me?"

She finally looks up. "Yes, baby?"

Straining on the ropes holding me to each bed post, I repeat, "You have to let me go." My eyes search her face for civility, but her lips don't move, her eyes are flat, and not a crinkle forms on her forehead.

She stops coating my injured skin, carefully closes the lid of the jar, places it back into the plastic kit, and snaps it shut.

One of her hands lifts my head while another draws the coffee mug to my lips. She shoves it against my mouth, willing me to open it, except I'm not interested in sampling any more of her concoctions.

My lips stay firmly pressed together and I twist my head away. She becomes more forceful until it feels like the porcelain is going to cut through my lips.

I open my mouth to get some relief. She pours some liquid inside and then pulls me in, coddling my face. The sugary coffee flavor coats my tongue, teeth, gums.

She takes a few long inhales from deep within her belly, like they teach you in yoga class. "God, you smell good." Her exhales are a loud growl. "Like rope burns and sex. My two favorite things."

She's vulgar. And so is her brew. I spit it out. The milky chocolate-colored liquid creates small puddles on her forearm.

Her grasp around me releases as she whisks off my spit with the sheet. My head falls back against the pillow with a discernible thump.

A click resounds in my ear and then cold, hard steel presses against my temple. Out of the corner of my eye I see a straight razor in her hand.

"Let's get something straight," she says, dragging the steel down the side of my face. "When you live under my roof, you follow my rules. You understand, baby?"

My breath hastens as the blade is pushed firmly into my cheek. Her blonde hair shadows her face and that musky perfume of hers inundates my nostrils...until I feel a prick go through my flesh.

I let out a yelp.

"You understand, baby?" she asks again.

"Ye...Yess," I stammer.

She slowly retracts the blade. "Good. Then I think this will work out just fine." She flips her hair back, composing herself, and holds the razor like a victory torch.

I watch her inspect her hand for long moment and then lick a trail of red from the side. "Mmm...the taste of a new lover, my third favorite thing."

The display makes my insides churn.

She slides off the bed and straightens out her shirt and skirt. "I'm going to be gone for a while. I have some...things...to clear up at work today, so that you and I can spend some more quality time together. You know, get to know each other better."

I tug at my restraints. My body aches from the prone position, and the fresh cut in my cheek sears. "Heather, please," I whimper, trying to find something human under the tough exterior as she walks away. "Please!"

She spins around and lunges at me.

I scream as the razor lands close to my face again. Her arm at my neck makes me cough. She brings the sharp blade to my eye level. I can tell she's enjoying watching the fear dance in my pupils, while hers continue to register solid blackness.

Satisfied that she's caused enough damage, she gets off me, saws through the rope binding one of my hands, and puts the razor into the front pocket of her hugging attire.

She walks to the front door and picks up a briefcase sitting near the exit.

"Why are you doing this?" I yell out, begging for some kind of sanity.

She stops and looks at me, fingering the key hanging on the chain around her neck. A genuine smile flashes across her face. "Because I need to."

She slips the key into the deadbolt and slides the door open.

Once she's outside, I hear it lock.

I touch my finger to my cheek. The blood is already drying.

EIGHT

When we started discussing what colleges I would apply to and what field of study I would take, I told my parents I was interested in becoming an astronaut. My mother immediately rebutted by telling me that I have never been good under pressure. That I quickly faltered and was unable to make snap decisions, and that I was prone to hysterics.

I wanted to argue that my hysterics were more tantrums caused by abandonment issues from my parents' hectic schedules and frequent traveling, but I doubted it would change her mind.

"That wouldn't make for much of an astronaut, now would it?" She phrased the question in her typical condescending tone. She'd always had her mind made up about me.

My father was more delicate about the matter, noting that I'd struggled with physics and didn't much like to drive, suggesting that perhaps I focus on subjects that came more naturally to me, like biology and chemistry. But then he added, "You'll do great at whatever you set your mind to" and gave my arm a squeeze, while my mother rolled her eyes.

I didn't hate my mother for constantly calling out my faults. She wasn't a delicate woman. She was driven by her research and career and the peers in her department, and I admired that. I just wondered why she'd ever bothered having a child. She didn't boast any maternal instincts.

Sometimes I would hurt myself, like purposely fall off my bike on a strip of road full of gravel, just to see if she would hurt too, or let me cry without making me feel like it was all my fault. But she didn't believe in giving blatant attention to a child. She'd probably think my being tied up here like this was some sort of stunt. It didn't matter. I'd given up trying to make her happy years ago, just like she'd given up trying to understand me.

My father asked me not too long ago during one of our weekly lunches if I was happy with the decision I'd made to be a molecular biologist. I knew what he was getting at, so I reassured him that becoming an astronaut had really been a stretch and that I'd figure out a different way to explore new territories. He stopped twisting the linguini around his fork and let it fall to his plate. He clutched his napkin and cleared his throat like he was about to convey something meaningful that I'd been waiting to hear my entire life… "I know you will, kiddo," he mustered and then picked up his fork again.

I look down at my naked body. My breasts sag to each side, my midsection is full of violent evidence, and my feet are red and puffy from cut-off circulation.

My lips tremble as I fight back tears. My mother is right. I am weak and not good in pressure situations. I never should have climbed back up the stairs. I should have not cared about the electronic leash I started carrying everywhere recently for the sake of finally having a boyfriend.

The blood pumps hard through my chest and every fiber ripples with adrenaline as I face the labels that have long been stapled to my forehead.

I need to get out of here. I don't know when she's coming back and I can't just lie here feeling sorry for myself. *I can get out of here,* I try to reassure my restless mind.

With my free hand, I stretch to untie the other. Fingers burn from grasping and tearing at the hemp. Tiny bristles burrow into my skin. Finally the knot loosens, and then releases. Relief comes over me as my arms drop naturally to their sides. I sit up carefully. My digits throb and my stomach is sore, as though I've done a thousand sit-ups. I reach delicately to untie each ankle.

Step one, done. I press my legs together and start kicking them, twisting my entire body. The silly sense of freedom makes me momentarily numb to any pain and doubt. I fall back on the bed and continue shaking the atrophy from my muscles.

My cell phone.

Step two. I throw the pillows off the bed.

It's gone.

I fumble around the sheets, but there's still no sign of it.

As I peer around the edges of the bed, I convince myself that she took it and it's now part of some ploy. Cutting me free from one of the ropes was probably a well-thought-out gesture as well.

And then I spot it. It's stuck between the ledge of the bed and the wall. I reach my hand through the thin space, scraping my skin against the brick, until I'm able to grasp it with the tips of my fingers. I begin lifting it out, cautious about not letting it drop further...until a door slam startles me.

I drop the phone.

She's home.

A strange flutter of adrenaline heats my insides. *What will she do to me when she sees what I've done?*

Slowly I turn around, convinced that I've lost whatever window of opportunity I had to escape.

Except I don't see anyone. How is that possible? Was it a neighbor? Did I imagine it? The four doors spaced equidistantly along one wall appear untouched.

My nipples harden from a strange anticipation and the hair on my arms stands. I need to get dressed.

Scurrying off the bed I limp around, searching for my clothes. Eventually I find my underwear, bra, tank top, skirt. They're thrown randomly around the couch.

It hurts to put everything back on, but it feels like a necessary part of a plan I haven't formulated yet. I scan the room for my purse, but it's not in an obviously visible spot.

I walk back over to the bed and crouch down to look under the massive steel frame. Dust fills my nostrils. I try not to breathe. I find my black wedges but no sign of my purse, or the phone that I let slip.

I crawl under the bed towards the brick wall, and when I reach it, I notice a deep crack in the wood floor. The light in the room hits the crevice just right and I peer down the slit.

My cell phone.

Except there's no way I'm going to reach it with my fingers. I'm going to need something long and thin and sturdy to extend my grasp. The battery's dead, but maybe I can figure out how to get a charge.

I inch my way out and sit up on my knees. My tank is covered in soot and my skin burns. I slip on the wedges I found moments ago. Forget the phone, and the purse, I just need to figure a way out.

Thump, thump, thump.

I turn to the four doors and this time listen harder and longer. The noises are definitely coming from behind one of them, and the only one I remember opening is the bathroom door on the far right. It's not like she gave me an official tour of her place.

As I walk closer to the four wooden access ways, I notice the portraits again. That first night they looked so artsy and erotic. The women appeared to be in throes of passion. Today, they look… captured.

An awful feeling grips me. I don't have time to investigate the sounds. I need to focus on getting out of here.

I turn for the front door of her loft, and when I reach it, I play with the deadbolt naively, thinking it might just loosen or maybe she didn't lock it quite right.

No dice.

I run my hands across the metal of the door, hoping to find some secret button that will unlatch it, but the brushed exterior feels inconspicuous to the touch. I grab the two-by-four that rests next to the door and ram it against the deadbolt, but manage only to get a few splinters wedged into my already-wounded hands.

I scan the countertop of her makeshift kitchen that starts right next to the door. There must be something I can use as a tool to pry open the lock. I touch my stomach. I *know* she has tools.

I pull the handle of each drawer and cupboard. Some don't open, and the ones that do are filled with nothing but plastic plates, cups, and utensils.

I walk to the toaster and try to move it, but it won't budge. I shove the coffeemaker and the same thing happens, even the dish rack won't shift an inch. There's not a loose item in sight and when I look closer, I discover everything is bolted down with large brackets and screws. *This is absurd. Who has everything bolted down?*

I reach for the handle of her refrigerator. Save for a couple six-packs of bottled beer, everything inside is neatly stored in plastic containers, stacked one on top of the other.

I slam the refrigerator door.

I kick a cabinet with the bottom of my wedge.

I kick it more, and more, and start cursing. "YOU FUCKING BITCH! YOU FUCKING INSANE SICK LESBIAN BITCH!"

I keep throwing everything I have into it, until I'm sweating and breathing hard and my body hurts even more and tears are streaming down my face again from frustration and pain.

"Bubblegum, bubblegum!" I scream, my insides about to combust. "Bubblegum, bubblegum!" I thump on the countertop, my head a mess of thoughts…

Janelle can't save me now.

I sink to the floor, near the dent I've made. I lift my hand to it and touch the blistered material, realizing I've not done myself any good. I pull the handle, thinking that if it opens, I can try to pop out the metal, but it's locked—just like most of the cupboards. I bury my head in my arms, more scared than I ever was in that crate when I thought some spirit from beyond was going to haunt me, knowing that if I don't pull myself together now, the consequences may be far more grave.

I heave myself up and fold over the sink. I turn on the cold water. It feels good on my swollen fingers.

I scoop up some water and splash my face, immediately feeling more human. I scoop more water and bring it to my lips this time, letting my tongue dip in and swallow. I stay hunched over the sink drinking water for a long time, not realizing how thirsty I've become.

The first-aid kit. Of course. There's got to be scissors or something in there I can use to pick the deadbolt or get my cell phone out.

I pat the excess water from my face and walk over to where Heather was playing nurse this morning.

Inside the plastic container, I find bandages, aspirin, and that ointment. I rummage around pointlessly, because there are obviously no scissors or surgical blades or anything that can help me.

My gaze falls on the only drawer of the end table, remembering it's where she retrieved the front door key from once…maybe there's a spare.

The wood slides unevenly, and it's hard to tell when the drawer is out as far as it will go. It's filled with odds 'n' ends. A couple of hair bands, a wad of tissues, some blank notepaper from the Biltmore Hotel, and an old manual camera.

It's an Olympus from the early eighties. My dad still uses his, even though he, too, has gone mostly digital. I take it out and play with the levers, surprised that after I press the shutter button I can hear film moving forward. Guess it's loaded. I focus the lens into the drawer, onto a bunch of crumpled receipts that mostly reveal Heather eats at restaurants and takes a lot of cabs.

One document in particular catches my eye, and I replace the camera in the drawer, running my fingers along the staple binding two sheets together. The top page is from the Los Angeles Superior Court, for a check Heather Thomas wrote for $50,000 to post bail. *Heather Thomas.* If only I could Google *that* right now… No wonder she couldn't be bought off. Looks like she makes plenty of money.

I flip to the next page and skim over a summary of charges from the State of California versus someone named Elisha Leger regarding illegal access to computer networks. *Why does she care to bail out a hacker?*

I shove the drawer closed, disappointed at not finding anything that can help my escape, and suspicious of the one drawer she decided to leave open. I walk over to the long wall of windows made up of individual panes. Some are open, but most aren't. I crank open the pane closest to me.

"Help!" I yell out desperately. "Somebody help me!"

Hearing nothing back, I peer out and look down and around. I'm surrounded mostly by brick and blue sky. "Is anybody out there?!"

The massive chopper blades of a helicopter swerve above me and I stick out an arm, waving ardently, wondering if this is someone coming to find me...until I realize it's foolish to think anyone can see me from that altitude.

Maybe if I break multiple panes and the wooden trusses between them, I can climb out. Except I'm at least ten stories up from the ground. Trying to scale my way down would be suicide. I would *definitely* fall.

Like my mother did one summer.

I'd just finished tenth grade and I lay under the orange tree in our backyard daydreaming about what I would do with all the spare time—what *Janelle* and I would do. Taking in the tree's thick, spicy aroma I glanced over at my mother. She was painting our home's exterior, standing on a tall ladder that ran all the way up to the second story. It wobbled because she'd set it on uneven ground, and I could see everything that was about to happen...even before she reached her paint brush for the edge of the window trim. Before she planted her foot in an awkward way.

Paint dyed the grass around me a robin's-egg blue. My mother cried out as her leg bent grossly sideways, then she hit the ground and lay trapped under the aluminum steps of the ladder, gasping.

The rumbling started deep in my gut. My body shook, and I had to bite the inside of my lips to keep from bursting into laughter. I couldn't explain my reaction. My hand quickly covered my mouth, but not before she noticed…that I hadn't rushed immediately to her aid.

I spent the rest of the summer paying for it. Forced to wait on her—and the cast attached to one leg—daily. A reason always materialized for not being able to visit with Janelle, including when her parents invited me to spend two weeks with them in Lake Tahoe and my mother told them she *needed* me at home.

I hated my mother. *And* her lectures about how careful I should be, especially when it came to friends. "Risky behavior doesn't pay off," she repeated all summer.

It turned out to be the summer before Janelle moved.

I hated my mother even more.

I shake off the memory and look down the brick wall outside of Heather's loft. I think I see a grate in the sliver of courtyard at the bottom, but I can't be sure. I can't be sure of anything except that it would qualify as "risky."

Where would I go even if I made it? There are no apparent doors, and everything through the few other windows looks abandoned. Heather's home isn't as cool and modern as I first thought. It's more the perfect human cage. I touch the frame of one of the windowpanes. I doubt if I can even break it.

I hear a loud crash—like a shelf with a bunch of glass has toppled over. Something is going on behind one of those four doors. I walk towards them, curiosity and fear filling my heart.

I put my ear to the door at center left. I hear some low whimpering, and not the kind a dog makes. When I pull on the knob, it doesn't open. I grab the knob of the door next to it. It opens into a large walk-in closet filled with racks and plastic bins. I move one of the racks away and press my ear against the wall.

Silence.

"Is someone in there?!" I yell, pounding my hand.

Not a peep.

I start thumbing through clothes hoping to find a metal hanger, something to crack the lock with, except everything is hung on various thicknesses of plastic.

I step out of the closet. The ruckus has stopped.

The air in the loft is perfectly still, except for the low hum of the ceiling fan, whose blades move like they're shouldering a heavy burden.

Confused, I move away, and decide to try the center right door.

It opens into a darkroom. The familiar smell of developing chemicals makes me smirk. Running my hand along the bins, I remember the hours my dad spent in his darkroom, especially when he returned from one of his and my mom's trips. When I was old enough, my dad taught me how to develop all the film they'd shot. He told me I picked it up fast and had a natural instinct for knowing just when to take out the photo to get the right exposure for the shot. That still means a lot to me.

Heather's bins are empty, and the wire where the photos should hang to dry is bare. Except for one piece. I unclip the roll of black-and-white negatives.

Two women laugh like old friends. One I recognize as Heather and the other is also blonde, except even taller and thinner. They look...normal. I wonder if these pictures were taken before

Heather went crazy, or maybe this is part of her crazy. The lure of normal, only to have it take an unexpected turn. I replace the film and walk further.

When I reach the back, I find another door. Instinctively I grab the knob, but it, too, is locked. My hands wander around the perimeter searching for another way to open it, until my gaze falls on a stack of photos piled in the corner.

They're close-ups of the other blonde. She looks scraggly and isn't laughing anymore. In one, she's screaming as if she's being terrorized, in another she's tied to some large plank, with red marks crossing her body, blood dripping out of some.

In another photo, her hair is splayed across a pillow and her eyes look ahead despondently into nothingness. Dark circles surround them. Her lips are slightly parted, and when I examine more closely, I see a faint dribble of something white.

I drop the stack of pictures and quickly tidy what I've touched.

Sick to my stomach, I back out into the loft and reach for the bathroom door. Within seconds I'm gripping the toilet and painfully vomiting out my insides. *Am I going to end up like the girl in the photos?*

I lift my head and flush the toilet. Exhausted, I place my hand on the edge of the claw-foot tub to pull myself to my feet. There's an undersized television hanging on the wall. A red light blinks on the side panel, as if it's turned on...or recording something.

Is she recording me? I jut out of view and look around her bathroom for more evidence of her spying on me, but don't find any.

My only impression is the same one I had when I first walked in a couple nights ago. It's not very clean. Not what you'd expect from a woman. Most women like to keep their bathrooms neat and tidy. They don't allow mildew to form along the tile, or let hair and dust build up along the floorboards, or let stains sit so long in the sink, you can barely scrape them off with your fingernails. According to my mother, anyway.

I rinse the putrid taste from my mouth and pick up a dirty razor that looks like a man's. The black and silver coating is nearly chipped off.

Has Heather ever had a man over here? I bet a woman like her doesn't even enjoy the company of a man. Unless it's to do to him what she did to that blonde girl…or what she's done to me.

I know there are women out there who don't like men. There are even women out there who have never been with a man. I met a girl like that last year. She was in my English Literature class and swore up and down she didn't care for anything without a cunt. She used those coarse words exactly and then invited me to go out with her that night. I told her I couldn't, so she suggested the next night and then the next.

I asked whether she was asking me out on a date. She looked at me like I was stupid, and the more we discussed it over the next few weeks, the more offended and angry she became until she eventually stopped coming to class.

Sometimes I regretted not going out on a date with her. I hadn't been on more than a handful of dates at that point, and I wondered if it would've been like going on a date with Janelle. No, I wasn't comfortable around her like I had been with Janelle. I wasn't even physically attracted to her.

Not like Heather.

Heather looked like a goddess at that club, with that wild mane of hair and glistening bronze skin over top those firm muscles. Her well-defined features exuded confidence, and those deep blue eyes commanded attention. She was everything I considered beautiful and sexy. And when she spoke, she had this elegant sophistication that made you believe every word she uttered and this persistence that made you want to say "Yes."

Just like Janelle.

Maybe that's how I ended up here. Doing all that *risky* stuff my mother would disapprove of. Maybe that's why I kissed Heather in the first place…because it'd been so long.

I drop the razor. Angry at myself for giving Heather the satisfaction of pleasant thoughts. I need to stay focused on how to get out of here, not wonder how I got *in* here.

She *has* to have something in her bathroom that I can use to pick the locks. I pull open every drawer and cabinet that will give and inspect the contents. But as with the kitchen, most everything is made of plastic. *Like she's prepared for my every move.*

Inside the medicine cabinet, I find lots of pills with names I don't recognize. Some of them look like prescriptions, but some have only handwritten labels that are hard to decipher. It also holds syringes and eye droppers and bottles with liquids in them and one pair of scissors—plastic, of course. From the look of Heather's medicine cabinet you'd think she has a degree in pharmaceuticals.

I hear the front door open with a loud rumbling and close the medicine cabinet swiftly.

NINE

"Well, I'm glad you didn't spend all day in bed," she says, sauntering slowly towards me after she's slid the front door closed and locked it with the key she keeps around her neck.

I can tell she's inspecting her place, and when she gets closer to me, she does the same.

"Heather, I want to leave."

She touches the strap of my tank top. "I think you'd feel a lot better if you got into some new clean clothes."

I shrug her hand away. "Heather, I'm serious. Please let me go."

"Or maybe you just need a bath," she continues, as if she hasn't heard a word I've said. "You like that claw-foot tub, don't you?"

She was watching me...recording me. I eye the key hanging around her neck and then I look towards the door. I should just grab it and bolt, right now. Maybe she won't even try to stop me and everything will be fine. Maybe I'll leave, and she'll just sit back and have a good laugh at the whole affair, and a few hours from now, I'll be back in my apartment thinking I overreacted. That she's not crazy and that I was never held against my will. That she's just a kinky bitch and this is how she gets off.

I summon every bit of courage I have and grab it. Ripping the chain from her neck, I run headlong for the front door.

A few strides in, I feel her tackle my feet. I topple forward, and as my hands try to brace the fall, the key and chain slide out.

She pins me, and I try to wrestle out from under her. My hand almost reaches the key again, but her frame is longer, and before long she's used the leverage of her wingspan to flip me over, kick my legs open, and pin my hands above my head.

"We can do this the easy way, Angie," I hear her grunt into my ear, "or we can do this the hard way." She pinches my wrists together.

"I don't want to do *anything* with you," I cry out, feeling fragile beneath her. "I just want to go home!"

Her hips grind heavily into my pelvis as she fumbles at her suit pocket with her free hand.

She whips out her cell phone near my face. "Isn't your boyfriend's phone number 310-554-5988?"

I freeze.

"That's what I thought," she says, her thumb now scrolling the screen of her phone. "You rocked my world last night. Can't wait to feel your cock inside me again," she reads from her phone. "You're addictive."

The sharp exhales through my teeth slow, as a mass of devastation expands in my throat, nearly choking me.

"I'm about to blow a load thinking about you. I'm dripping

right now—Erik." She lays a heavy accent on his name. "Do you really need to hear any more of this sexting, because it *does* go on, and on, or are you ready to accept that a little time apart from your cheating boyfriend might do you some good?"

I thrust upwards, trying to buck her off me. "I don't believe you! You're making it up just to keep me here."

Her chest sinks into mine, making it hard to breathe. "You came home with me for a reason, Angie. You wanted to learn something about yourself. I don't have to make up some exorbitant lie to make you stay. You want to stay." She loosens her grip around my wrists. "*You* know that craving you felt, and the anticipation, and then when I finally touched you…" Her fingers drag slowly down my arms and sides. "And let you unleash…" She grabs firmly onto my hips. "You know that was just the tip of the iceberg and there's so much more for us to explore."

Flashes of the last forty-eight hours replay in my mind. Watching her dance, the thrill of letting loose with her, the incredible orgasm. But then she tied me to her bed, and those prophetic photos, and the taser…

"You drugged me. And hurt me—"

"How do you think we learn about ourselves, Angie? By being comfortable and not pushing our boundaries? By always feeling safe?" Her lips pause at my chin and the smell of coffee is heavy on her breath. "You want to go home? Believe his excuses and go back to status quo? That's always going to be there for you. But this, and me…if you walk away now, you may regret it forever. What's a couple more days?"

I go limp under her. My emotions completely torn. How can I trust a woman who has threatened my life? And yet there's truth in her words.

"Whose phone is that?" I ask meekly.

She rolls off me and sits up on her knees, after grabbing the key from the floor. "Don't worry—I'm not fucking your boyfriend. I've got a friend on the inside who traced his number and forwarded me all his text messages over the last few weeks. After *you* confided he'd been acting strange."

The tone in her voice makes me feel almost guilty for doubting her motives as anything but good—even though I know that's ridiculous. Her "friend" is probably the hacker she bailed out.

She offers me her hand. "I'm looking out for you," she says, as if it's something obvious I've overlooked in my assessment of our time together.

Still uncertain, I take her hand and she pulls me up to stand. With one arm cradling me, she walks us away from the front door over to her couch. She tells me to sit and then goes into her closet.

One by one, the racks and bins start coming out, as thoughts of Erik's betrayal run through my head. I shouldn't be surprised that he hooked up with some other girl. Literally packs of groupies go to all the water polo games, and his friends always have girls hanging on them, and they're always pretty. I've never felt like I could compete with any of that, despite Erik's reassurances. It was stupid of me to think we had a real shot.

"Lighten up, Angie," Heather interrupts my thoughts. "Let's have some fun." She pulls me to stand. "No better way to get back at someone than to beat them at their own game." She hands me a corset with intricate beadwork and sequins, and then opens the lid of another bin and pulls out a set of white wings made of beautifully strewn-together feathers.

"What's all this for?" I don't feel even slightly enthusiastic about playing dress-up right now.

She places the wings next to me and gently touches my shoulder. "Helping you explore who you are on the inside. In a safe place."

I worry about what she presumes I've agreed to, and highly doubt that there is *anything* safe about this place. I tell her I have class on Monday, but the way she ignores that statement makes me feel like I don't have much of a choice.

She starts going on about how stifling it is—ninety-three degrees according to her thermostat—and how all the drama has made her work up a sweat. It's made her terribly thirsty. She takes off her blazer and throws it on the couch and then does the same with her blouse.

I notice she's wearing a similar corset to the one I'm holding except it's black.

She walks to her fridge and bends over. The back of her skirt is slit high up her hamstrings. They're perfectly toned and tanned. She looks back at me. "Want a beer?"

I shake my head.

"It'll help you relax," she pressures.

I give her the same response, still leery of her intentions.

She shrugs her shoulders in a suit-yourself manner and twists the top off her beer.

She gingerly takes a sip, throwing her head back in relief, and then unzips her skirt and lets it fall to the floor. The straps of a black garter belt dangle loosely and the muscles in her long legs pop as she walks back over to me in her tall heels. The sight of her near-naked torso distracts my scattered thoughts.

She pulls me from the couch and offers to help me change, as if she knows I'll fumble. Before I have a chance to answer, I feel her hand slide off the straps of my tank top and unclasp my bra. I close my eyes tightly, feeling even more self-conscious than usual, knowing my body is marked with scars from last night and that hers looks flawless.

Nothing seems to deter her. She strokes the underside of my breasts with purpose, grazing her thumbs around my nipples until they harden.

"You're breathtaking, Angie," she flatters as she reaches around back and unzips my skirt.

Don't let it go to your head. She's probably just baiting you.

After a few tugs, my skirt lands on the ground. I imagine the whiteness of my thighs and the cellulite I've been burdened with since junior high school and how it must look so unsavory, but she takes my hand in hers and guides it down her body...

Oh god.

I'm on her pubic mound, my fingers feeling that coarse hair, and then I'm at her folds, my fingers now feeling the sticky wetness.

"You can't fake excitement."

My eyes pop open and my hand retracts.

She takes a gulp of her beer and sticks the sweating bottle between my breasts. The cold is startling, but she continues to hold the glass against my skin, moving it slowly down my belly, until it reaches my underwear. I press against it.

"That feels good, doesn't it?" she whispers. "But you know I can do a lot better than that."

Her words make my insides clench.

She takes another long swig from her beer before placing it on the floor and lifting the white corset.

She helps me into it, folding the rigid material around my midsection and cinching it tight at my back. My frumpy underwear is replaced with a tiny thong, and the hooks of the garter belt are snapped into the silky white stockings she patiently slides my legs into. Only the white patent stilettos with silver studs on the toe and heel remain…and of course the wings. I slip carefully into these last bits as though I'm in the midst of a balancing act.

Once Heather's satisfied with my appearance, I watch her work on hers until we're standing across from one another, mirror images except I'm in virgin white and she suitably drips black.

She walks into the darkroom and after a few minutes emerges with her control box, a video camera, a tripod, and a wooden box.

The blinds whirl down to rid the room of all natural light, and a flood of royal blue envelopes us. She sets the camera on the tripod and then walks back over to where I'm standing.

She reaches into one of the plastic bins again and pulls out two masks. The white Mardi Gras–style mask goes over my face, and the black one over hers.

"Now you can express whatever you feel on the inside without worrying what it looks like on the outside."

The red light of her video camera turns on.

She tells me to walk towards it.

I comply, but feel wobbly in footwear I'm not used to.

"Stop," she orders. "Get down on all fours."

I slowly sink, my knees hitting the concrete. I'm glad to not have to walk further, but anxious about what she has in mind.

The small wooden box sits in front of me until she takes it out of view, but I can sense her with it behind me. It has a scent of dried, pungent flowers. It reminds me of a perfume my mother used to wear. I dare not turn around or rub any of the discomfort from my knees. I hear the clicks of the box opening and closing.

Finally, her hands glide over the exposed parts of my behind. My pulse quickens and my hands sweat.

Her fingers playfully pull on the string of my thong, scalloping into the creases of my lower lips. My body awakens with the same lust I felt the first night she made advances toward me.

Methodical, come-hither motions target my most vulnerable parts, and my back arches, guiding her to give me more.

She works my opening. Slowly stretching it, moving her finger in and out of it, while her thumb nips at my clitoris.

The wetness seeps through what little fabric constructs my underwear. Everything continues to become more slick and sensitive.

I fall in line with her rhythm, my mind a slave to her touch, forgetting all her ruthless behavior as if it were something of little consequence. The pressure builds and I wish it to quicken.

"Not so fast," she chides, pulling away from me.

The sudden detachment is grinding, but moments later I feel something push at my opening. It's round, smooth-textured, cool, and definitely has some weight to it. It's medium-sized, if I were to wrap my palm around it. I feel it push inside me, and when it pops in, I convulse around its heaviness.

Moments later, another similar object is at my sex. This one glides up and down, teasing me, until I'm on an unbearable edge.

When it breaks in, the two weights fill me in a different way than Erik's cock. They nudge at spots inside of me I've never felt, and I squeeze, wanting to extract more sensation.

"Crawl towards the camera," her voice commands.

I have to think about what she's saying. I've forgotten there's a camera recording.

I look up at the device, comforted by the fact that my face is covered with a mask. I tepidly make my start, kneecaps crunching against an unyielding floor, balls inside me willing a desire to unleash…

A sting lands on my right thigh.

I yelp in surprise.

Another strike lands on my behind and she yells at me to keep crawling.

Everything in my well-educated mind tells me that this should hurt, that I should protest her assault, but instead the balls inside me feel fuller and I let out an unexpected groan, heeding her command.

The red light of the camera burns a hole through my previously clear vision. As I near it, my hips sway more flagrantly and my lips part so I can lick them. I cock my head, as if the camera is coming alive, as another smack, and then another, and another, each one harder, puts me on an emotional cliff.

My back twists and I swivel around like a horse with a long, elegant tail. Insides clenched in pleasure and a tear rolling down my face, but not from any physical pain—from the realization that I'm doing something I've never done before and allowing myself to completely enjoy it instead of feeling ashamed like I have in the past.

Chest heaving and hips burning, any admonishing or contentious inner voice escapes further from reach with each blow. When I turn around, the devil smiles back as if she knew how I would react all along.

I'm so close I could knock over the camera, but I don't want to.

The lashing ends.

Her hands move slowly all over my entire back side. They feel like silk, like nobody's hands have ever felt on my body. They caress and tease near my sex, my insides continuing to milk those balls, driving me to a brink that I need to get over.

I buck harder, begging for the release.

She grabs my hair and her fingers are once again at that spot. Those motions…back and forth, back and forth against my clit, in that steady rhythm that may never end, unless I give into it.

The climax comes like a vicious master, from a place not built on logic or reason, but one that has forgotten the difference between right and wrong, taking my body to the outer reaches of the life I've been living, making me doubt whether I ever want to go back.

TEN

Heather is not going to work today. Instead she tells me we need to rehearse and then reaches into her pocket, grabs a very full key ring, and opens that door I couldn't yesterday. That door I heard all those noises behind.

I want to follow her in and ask her what she's hiding, but I can't. She's bound me in leather cuffs to an old radiator that looks like it hasn't been used in thirty years.

At first I thought it was because she didn't believe I'd stay on my own accord, regardless of what I agreed to or how she's been able to summon my body to pleasure. But now I realize that these are her preferred house rules. She wants me to stay put and not think about anything—to control me. Wait for her to arrange and organize and take care of everything, including my thoughts.

I half expect an army of sexual submissives to rush out of *that* room, bend to their knees, and offer up their most sacred of parts. The way I did last night.

I've researched the traits of dominance and submission. It's one of the more interesting things I've done in school. It happened last year, after I saw something on the Internet that sexually stimulated me in an embarrassing way. I started poring over everything I'd learned. Re-reading theories on epigenetics and molecular genetics and genomic imprinting to see if I could find a biological link.

Certainly there were plenty of examples of sub-dom relationships in the animal kingdom, and mutations in the dopamine receptors did lead to some of us being less averse to fear and pain. But now I realize that maybe it's far simpler than all that. That maybe what I watched just once but ended up replaying in my mind over and over was purely a sexual preference I'd never realized about myself or wanted to admit to before.

I watch her tug on a large prop. Like the pommel horse you're taught to swivel on in gymnastics class, except this one's more sinister. It's made of dark wood and cowhide, and adorned with shackles, chains, and levers.

My armpits grow moist and beads of sweat begin to trickle, because today there is especially little air moving through her expansive space. I try to get comfortable in the corner as she checks the monster for defects. My mind races, torn between thoughts of escape and a growing sexual appetite that has nothing to do with the fact that since I arrived, she's fed me only some buttered toast and steamed white rice with a slab of butter on top.

Pleasure, I am learning, is a curious thing. Those who on the surface look to be our best match are sometimes unable to get any great physical reaction, regardless of how hard they try, while those that you know offer no future sometimes understand our bodies the way no one else can.

She wipes down the leather. "I want to make sure it's comfortable for you."

The thought of her doing something to me on that big, hard prop makes me dizzy.

She takes a few strides towards me and squats down to my eye level. "What's wrong, baby? Not into it?" She pulls on the tank top that reeks of unwashed days. "Or are you?" Her voice softens. "No need to be embarrassed. A lot of people are surprised by what they like."

My stomach churns. *What's happening to me?*

I look into those dark blue eyes of hers that never give away anything more than what she wants you to see.

"You can't make me like everything." It's all I can think to say to keep some semblance of control in the situation.

Her smile widens. "You'd be surprised at what I can make you like."

She yanks on one of my cuffs, willfully hurting me, and reaches into her pocket for the large set of keys. She flips through them until she finds the right one, and forces the cuff around my wrist closer to her so that she can jam a key into the side.

It opens. My hands are freed and she tugs me to stand, aggressively pulling me over to the black monster.

Fight her! Punch her, kick her, scratch her, pull her hair, claw at her face. Do something to let her know you haven't completely succumbed. But I don't want to jeopardize my departure. It's just one more day.

She pushes me against the prop and tells me to climb on. The leather at my chest feels like a muscular torso ready to be put to any task. Her body presses up against mine. The thickness of the hide makes my skin sweat more, and her hips dig into my rear, letting me know who's in charge.

She starts heaving me up, and with the friction from both sides…it feels like a part of me will rip. I grab onto two levers jutting out from the sides as she gives me one last push up and forward.

Quickly she moves to shackle my wrists and ankles to the horse—like a warrior about to go to battle, making sure I'm securely in place. And then she stops.

I must have a defeated look on my face because she starts to caress me. Pacing backwards to rub my back, telling me everything is going to be alright.

"You look too warm," she suddenly frets, walking into her bathroom. Moments later, she comes out with a face cloth and a small pan of water. She dips the towel until it's fully submersed and takes it back out, squeezing the extra liquid from the fabric.

She slides the cold towel over my skin, relieving my body temperature and wiping away the excess grime that's collected from not showering in days. The pseudo-sponge bath feels divine. It's almost as if some semblance of a conscience has risen from deep within the beast. The coarse towel texture makes the fine hairs of my follicles stand, and her plying fingers release the tension in my muscles, blurring the lines again between fear and lust.

She continues to alternate between refreshing the towel and tending to my body. "Are you thirsty?"

I nod.

She starts chewing a nail again before remembering her manicure and pulling her finger out of her mouth. "I'm sorry. I—"

The empathy in her tone and disposition puzzles me. In the short time I've known her, Heather has never been at a loss for words. She backs up and turns for the kitchen.

When she returns with a bowl of ice water, I realize that all of this might scare her as much as it scares me. Even though it's more familiar, it can't be any easier. Whatever she's doing...she must know she's treading a dangerous line. Maybe she's already crossed it. She holds the bowl in front of my mouth. I lap it up like a dog, glad for the hydration.

"Thank you," I say, and then try to shake off some lethargy from my bones. But the binds are too restrictive. "Heather?"

She puts down the water bowl. "Yes?"

"Tomorrow is the end of the arrangement. The end of the two days you asked me to stay. Are you going to let me leave?"

The question stiffens her, as if she expected her kind gestures to give us a few extra days together, but that's not the point. I need to know she wasn't lying to me.

She takes out the large key ring and shakes it in front of my face. Her fingers flip through the keys aggressively until they land on one.

"What are you doing?" I demand, watching her pull the key through the loop, separating it from the rest.

"You want to leave?" The remaining keys drop to the floor like the crashing of cymbals as she walks to the kitchen area. I see her dangle the lone key over the sink. "Sure, Angie. You can leave. Unless…it's not meant to be."

The key falls from between her fingers.

My eyes widen as I watch her flip a switch. Loud noises of metal wearing on metal fill the room, and my body doesn't feel cool or comforted anymore.

I scream at her that she can't be trusted. That she's unstable and needs help. I beg her to stop manipulating me and let me go… but just then, our interlude is broken by a knock at the door.

She freezes.

I can tell by her expression that she's as surprised as I am by the intrusion. My heart thumps faster. Could it be Erik? Did he get my text messages? Did someone hear my calls for help? I feel my survival mechanism kicking in again and scream at the top of my lungs, "Help me! Help me please! I'm inside and I've been kidnapped!"

She stomps towards me, her eyes filled with fury, as if *I've* betrayed *her*. As if *she's* the one being held hostage to someone else's will. I hear porcelain shatter as she kicks the water bowl near me, and I continue to scream. She reaches for something under the prop.

It slams against my mouth and an elastic band snaps at the back of my head. My teeth and lips throb from the impact and my screams become muffled.

The knock at the door becomes an insistent banging. She moves away from me and after a few seconds I hear her ask, "Who is it?"

From behind the door someone calls out that it's the city inspector.

"What do you want?" she continues yelling through the door.

This time there's no answer, but the banging continues. I hear her unlock the deadbolt and the male voice again. "What's going on in there?"

It's definitely not Erik.

I strain to look behind me and see who it is, but she's got the door slid open only a crack and is holding the two-by-four that always rests next to it.

"I'm busy," she snaps back.

I try to make noise through my gag.

Please don't leave! Please notice I'm here. I start babbling and screaming again, though I know it's all too obscure, especially from this far away.

"Busy? For me?" The voice sounds more brutish this time.

"Busy right now," she answers.

I hear her struggle to keep whoever is on the outside from coming inside, and when I look back again, I see an arm trying to push its way through the door.

An ill thought crosses my mind. If she doesn't want this person in here, maybe I don't want him in here either.

"This is *our* time," he says louder, with more venom.

"I know," she grunts, as she manages to wedge the two-by-four in the rail, "but I have something else going on at the moment."

"Something else going on?" he repeats dumbly.

"Yes, I'm working." Her voice is irritated. "You know, work? The whole reason I need this space. You're going to have to come back later."

"But this is our time."

He batters the door, trying to use his might to slide it further, but her two-by-four won't allow it.

"Yes, and normally our time together takes precedence, but today is different."

"But we have an arrangement," he cries out like a brat.

"I have other arrangements too, and you caught me in the middle of one, and I can't just stop. Understand?"

Silence fills the room.

"Can I watch?" His tone is softer now.

The thought makes me sick. It's one thing to deal with *her* twisted fantasies, it's another to deal with someone else's too. I can't trust her to protect me. I try to flap my arms and legs, hoping she didn't completely lock one of the shackles that binds me to her monster prop, but nothing gives.

They argue some more, because she tells him he can't watch and to come back another time.

But he won't stop. "It's not easy to find the time to come out here, I can't just come and go…"

I look back again to see his one hand still grabbing the edge of the door. "Now is the only time!" He starts rattling the door.

I panic, wondering if the two-by-four will be able to hold him off much longer.

She stops bracing the door.

I watch her adjust her white denim shorts and her purple strapless top. She fluffs her hair out before peering through the slot she's allowed. "So our time together isn't worth waiting for?" There is a change in her tone. "*I'm* not worth waiting for?"

His rumbling stops. "No…you are. I just—"

"I always do my best to accommodate you. And now all you care about is that it's convenient for you?" Her voice cracks, like she's about to cry. "I mean so little to you that you can't understand this one time?"

The city inspector stops trying to open the door. He murmurs an apology.

It's not good enough for her.

She slides the door violently.

I hear him yell out and curse, painfully retracting his hand.

"When I say come back, you come back! You understand?" she bellows, and then the deadbolt clicks.

She marches toward me and bends down so we're eye to eye. Beads of sweat run across her brow, and she's breathing heavily. "Some people just don't get it."

She pulls the gag out of my mouth and throws it to the floor. Her hands are shaking.

She starts pacing and then rummages through a pile of clothes in a corner until she finds what she's looking for.

Fanning her face with one hand, she lights up a joint with the other. She inhales deeply several times, until her hands stop trembling, and then offers it to me. I shake it away. She brings the tripod and video camera closer and presses the record button.

The joint dangles from her mouth as she reaches for the camera she likes taking pictures with and points it at my face.

She starts clicking.

I turn my head, trying to avoid both lenses. "I don't want to take pictures right now."

"God, you're great in front of the camera." She ignores me again and continues to snap pictures, trying to distract herself, and me, but the pieces of the puzzle are suddenly coming together.

She's not an artist like she claims to be. She probably didn't even go to UCLA. She's not a businesswoman paying her bills and way through life. She's not trying to get me to open up so that she can capture some sequence of emotions in time, or prove some point to me about love or relationships. She just uses whatever is left of her body and looks and graces to get whatever she needs to survive.

"And you're a whore."

The camera stops snapping.

"You have sex with him so you can live here." Her face pales. "You're even sicker than I thought." I wonder how many more arrangements she has like this.

She steps away from me and takes another hit off her joint. "I use him the way he wants to be used."

"People don't mean anything to you. That's why you're a whore."

Her smack comes hard across my face, but I don't care. I refuse to let her manipulate me anymore with her lies.

"He's important. Our relationship is complicated," she defends and smacks me across the face again. My other cheek burns.

She lets go of the camera and lifts my chin. One of her fingers begins to trace the outlines of my features, more firmly with each stroke. "Such a pretty girl." Her hand cups around my neck forcing my head back further and further, until it feels like she wants to snap it off. "Why would she try to hurt me?"

Her trajectory is stopped by pounding at the door again.

She lets go of my neck and extinguishes the joint on the floor. The gag goes back into my mouth.

This time she grabs a long metal prod on the way to the entrance and makes sure the two-by-four is securely in place before slowly opening the deadbolt.

"I told you, now is *not* a good time!" She plays tough again, but this time a mallet drives through, hitting the edge of the door, shattering the two-by-four, sliding it open.

Heather falls backwards and hits the floor. The metal prod bounces from her hand. I can't tell if she's been hit or not.

The mallet swings several more times and the man on the other side tears through like a raging bull.

He's tall and thick, and wears grey slacks and a white shirt with the sleeves rolled up. Under different circumstances, one might consider him an attractive and robust older man. The veins pop out of his forearms, the salt-and-pepper hair falls into his eyes, and a fistful of chest hair protrudes above the top button of his shirt. He stands open-mouthed, cursing and swinging his mallet over her. She looks tiny in the wake of his entrance.

For an instant, I think he's going to kill her—just bash her brains in right there—and I nervously think he'll probably do the same to me, but she leaps from the ground. I see her rush for the stun gun she mounted on a charger earlier in the day near the kitchen area.

She reaches for her weapon, but his large hands grab the back of her shirt, tearing it and flinging her. She bounces off the butcher block table, toppling the stools around it.

He looks over to me, prone and shackled to the horse, and then to the camera. Its red dot pins me like a sight on a rifle.

"You want *her* more than me?!" He wraps a meaty hand around Heather's neck and picks her up. Her bandeau-style bra barely holds up. I hear her choking and trying to cough. They walk like this in my direction. Her feet kick at him, but the large man barely notices.

"*I* let you live here! Not her!" he roars, knocking her torso so hard into the monster prop I'm shackled to, it creaks and sways. "Me!" He continues to jostle her like a rag doll.

My right side is getting battered, and my pleas for him to stop are hopelessly lost through the object still lodged in my mouth.

The leather buttress continues to heave until I hear the crack of wood and feel myself falling. The left side of my body hits the floor hard and the impact leaves me dazed.

"It's always been up to me!" I hear him go on, even though my ears ring, my head pounds, and the suffocating heat makes me feel close to passing out...

Something lands heavily and the floor beneath me quakes.

A bolt of adrenaline rushes through my veins, forcing me to lift my head.

She's on her back. Her legs are kicked apart and he's dropped between them. He lifts his fist.

"It's me," I hear her meek voice say. "It's me, baby."

He stops whatever he's about to unleash on her.

I watch like a spectator at the gladiator games, my heart pounding in my throat.

She continues to talk him down, until he retracts his fist and lowers himself to her. Locked in her hypnotic gaze. It looks like they're about to kiss, and I wonder if this is part of some sick lovemaking ritual, until I see her snap up with a strong head-butt.

He tries to shake it off, but she slaps both her hands over his ears and then sends a hard heel-palm into his nose. The large man sways, stunned.

I hear her laugh sadistically.

He bends his torso back, like he's about to hit her, but instead takes his belt off his worn pants.

He holds the belt high in the air and when he strikes her, she lets out a shriek that pierces the air like a cat in an alley fight. I turn my gaze away, unable to watch.

"Whatever you want to do!" I hear her yell out in a reverent voice.

He drops his belt and puts his hands on her white bottoms, gazing at them like a precious jewel.

"It's up to you." Her voice is wispy and permissive.

He tears her shorts open, unzips his fly, and pulls out his organ.

"It's up to you." Her fists relax, and for a moment they curl around his hard unit, as if she's admiring it, forgetting she's supposed to be defending herself. The way I did.

He groans before swatting them away, and she slashes at him with her paws. *What are they doing?*

I glance at the opened door, freedom calling to me, and focus on breaking my bonds before the pair loses their fascination with one another.

My left thigh and arm are pinned, but I can tell that from this angle, I may be able to break the two pieces of wood holding my shackles in place. I lift my right leg so that the piece of wood is vertical and push down on the leather trunk of the horse. I hear it crack, but it's not enough.

I see her try to turn over and crawl away, but he pulls her under him and drives himself into her. As his grunts become more feverish with each thrust, her cries become more like groans.

I hoist up the horse again, the leather slipping between my sweaty palms. This time, I ram it down as hard as I can and it breaks the wood. The plank holding my ankles breaks in half.

He pins her wrists above her head with one hand and cups her throat with the other, the way she did mine. I hear her gasp for air, which only makes him ride her harder and tighten his grip.

Their bodies expand and contract in unison until her eyes start to glaze over. Sputters of air release from her mouth as he hikes her legs around his beefy arms so he can take her deeper, putting himself over the edge. He shudders with orgasm, exploding into her, and then slumps over.

Their sordid ritual is over.

His fingers gently caress her face as if trying to express some ill-defined and repented emotion. Then he lifts himself and zips up.

I close my eyes and pretend to be unconscious. Clasping onto the leather prop, hoping it will somehow protect me.

I hear his long gait stride across the room, each foot falling loudly on the cement floor, increasing in volume as he approaches me. He stops, and I can smell his pungent odor and hear his hoarse, winded breath.

I try to make the air coming through my lungs as shallow as possible.

After a few beats, I hear him walk away, his footsteps becoming fainter until nothing remains but the sound of the fan blades overhead sweeping the air in the room again.

Swallowing a large gulp of air, I peek out.

Heather is lying on the floor, catatonic. I'm not sure she's even alive. But he's definitely gone.

The door is still open.

I push the leather horse off me and use both feet to break the wood holding my wrists in place.

I struggle to my hands and knees and start crawling, pieces of metal and wood dragging behind me. I have to stay focused on my escape, but I can't help but look back. Her legs are splayed open, her arms still above her head, and her clothes are ripped on all sides.

Part of me wants to check on her. Help her. I know there's still something good in her. I can tell from the way she wants me to experience pleasure. There's an altruistic prodding, patience, and understanding. But there's as much horror as there is allure on the canvas she's painted. Probably too much for me to ever blend into something beautiful.

I continue to the door.

A sense of relief fills me as I reach the barrier. I grasp onto the ledge and pull myself to stand, my breathing sharp and my limbs heavy. I take in a lungful of air, wanting my body to run, but it's taken too many physical and emotional hits. The best I can do is carefully reach one foot acro—

Fingers grip tightly around my ankle and yank me back.

I stagger, reaching out for anything, something, trying to hold my balance, but start falling to the floor.

Now she's on top of me, all her body weight smothering me again. I feel the probes of the stun gun on my torso.

"I'm curious," she whispers in my ear. "Just now, making it to the door…what were you thinking?"

I can barely catch my breath, the shock and physical pain overwhelming me, the promise of freedom drifting away.

"I was thinking it was over," I finally manage to say.

"Not even close."

The stun gun digs deep into my rib cage, and I know she's about to pull the trigger.

"Wait!" I summon a voice and courage that comes from a place of resolution. "It's me. It's me, baby." I clutch onto her, fingers digging deeply so she can register that they're real. "I'm not leaving." I pull her in harder, trying to envelope every last broken bit of her.

She stops whatever she's about to unleash on me.

"Whatever you want to do."

My mouth finds hers and fervently commands her attention until our eyes lock into an understanding. "It's up to you," I say.

The stun gun drops away from my side and she rolls off me.

We lie panting…

ELEVEN

I wake from a fitful sleep, stepping through desires that make my body ache, and horrors that shake my core, until I open my eyes to find the last rays of light cascading through the windows. I roll to my side and pull a pillow into me, noticing loose ropes around my wrists.

The whirl of a drill startles me. I look over my shoulder to find her hunched over a workbench. She's fixing the pieces of wood I snapped in half and screwing the shackles back into place.

I look down at my ankles to find they also have rope around them, with just as much lag. It's more of a gesture today than a command. I could untie myself easily, but I don't. Instead I sit up and watch her work, amazed at the vigor with which she's putting that monster prop back together, beat up as she is.

It's as if the motions of picking up and straightening out everything that's been pummeled apart are going to mend whatever has been broken inside. Or maybe the act I witnessed yesterday has become routine and this is part of a customary clean-up.

I feel sorry for her. I know I shouldn't. I know what she's capable of regardless of my growing curiosity.

She finishes tidying up her place with such meticulous care, little evidence remains of what's taken place. Unless you looked at *our* battle scars. I lean to my side and a dull pain shoots through my torso.

She walks over and sits down next to me. "Angie, I'd like you to get back on the whipping bench," she says matter-of-factly, as if whatever we were about to do yesterday had been interrupted by nothing more than a phone call.

I don't respond. *So that's what it's called.* The literal meaning sinks in and that fear and anticipation begin to mix together again into an addictive drug.

"There's so much I want you to experience."

It scares me to imagine what that means in her world, yet it makes a part of me feel special too. She wants to take me on a journey. I always thought I'd do that with Erik, but there hadn't been enough time...and maybe there never will be. Maybe he's already decided to do that with someone else.

When she asks again, I offer up my hands.

I can tell she's surprised, because she takes her time drawing all the rope off me, looking at me like she's expecting me to change my mind. But when I don't, the tension between us eases.

We walk over to the familiar prop, and she tells me to wait while she gets something. When she returns with that something, I have no idea what it is, except for a bunch of leather straps with buckles and rings.

"It's a body harness," she answers my confused expression. "I want you to put it on."

I imagine the firm leather denting into my plump flesh, old insecurities playing with my mind again, but her fingers are already lifting the tank top off me and pulling down my underwear. I avoid her gaze as she pulls the harness around the front side of my body.

One strap sits above my breasts, another below, and one down the center. When she buckles it tight at my back, I let out a gasp, and when she pulls the last strap between my legs and attaches it at my behind, I feel those sensations again from deep inside. *Why does this turn me on so much?*

She tells me that something's missing and then cups each of my breasts for a moment before disappearing again. When she reappears, it's with two small clamps. She adjusts them around my nipples…just tight enough to make me twinge. A long chain hangs between them, and when she gives it a light tug, a sweet warmth rushes between my thighs.

"What do you think?" she asks with a spark in her eyes.

I blush and bite at my lower lip, not wanting to tell her that it's making me hot. I like her like this. With a certain naiveté that makes me confident she has no ulterior motives.

She pats the bench, silently prodding me to get on. I swing one leg over so that my body can straddle the large prop, wondering if I've lost my mind. This is the type of thing I once heard some girls snickering about in the library. Weird, kinky stuff that old rich men wanted to do with them. Gross, they said. A shopping trip and private jet ride wasn't nearly enough compensation—as if we were all getting offers like that. Leave it to the prostitutes and porn stars, they added.

They're wrong, I think as the tips of her fingers run between the leather and my skin, making sure the tension is just right. This has nothing to do with compensation, and everything to do with bravely exploring who you really are. She rubs my wrists and ankles with that same ointment she used on my stomach a few days earlier, and the heavy bonds go back on. These ones don't have as much lag. She locks them, securing me in place, and then walks into the bathroom. I'm brimming with anticipation of what's to come.

She holds out two pills and some water. "Don't worry, just painkillers," she tries to reassure me. "We both took quite a beating. This'll take the edge off."

Not quite what I had in mind.

I watch her pop one of the pills in her mouth—as if to earn my trust.

I open my mouth, putting faith in the promise.

She places the remaining pill on my tongue and then tips back the water cup against my lips so I can swallow.

It makes her happy when I'm obedient. It also gives me back some power.

She prances over to where a light trench coat hangs and slips it on, as well as a pair of black patent heels. She slings a large black bag over her shoulder and almost sings when she tells me she has to step out for a while.

When I ask her where she's going and when she'll be back, she tells me to revel in this time away from responsibility and relax. She plays with a video camera off to my side. "Everything feels better after a good rest" are her parting words before the door slides closed.

I turn my head away from the camera, feeling the firm leather of the horse against my cheek. *I suppose she's right.* My thoughts begin to quiet and my body starts to numb. Even though I've just woken up, I realize how little sleep I've gotten over the last four days and eventually drift off...

The air feels cooler when I awake this time, like the heat has finally broken. I'm startled by how empty the loft feels and call out her name. No response. *How long is she planning on leaving me like this?* I try to lie calmly, but now I am wide awake and with each passing minute getting more restless.

By the time I notice the first traces of light in the loft, I've decided that her test of patience is actually a form of punishment. *What have I done wrong now?* I've darn near obeyed her every whim the last twenty-four hours.

My mother would do this type of stuff when she was really mad. Never let me know exactly why her demeanor had taken such a terrible turn or how I could fix it. She'd just lock me in my room until she decided she was ready for me to come out. I remember those stressful hours that would sometimes border on a complete day. Making lists of all the reasons why I was such an inadequate daughter.

I turn to the red light of the video camera. "You're just trying to mess with my mind! Freak me out, get me all riled up, make me feel insecure, so that I can what…obey you even more?!"

The room suddenly feels like my old bedroom, with its teen heartthrob posters that my mother thought I should be interested in and nondescript contemporary furniture and hangers full of clothes I'd never properly fit into and the Anne Rice novels that I'd store in a dissection toolbox under my bed because I knew my mother would never open it.

I glare at the video camera. "Except that I'm a lot smarter than you've ever given me credit for!" I yell at it like I've always wanted to at my mother. "I had a whole stash of Oreos and Skittles and Pringles in a shoebox in my closet that you never found. You'd never starve me, even though I know you wanted to."

I'm panting and sweating, realizing that my adolescence was such a cliché. I could've starred in my own self-help book.

Finally, a door opens, though it's not the metal clang of the large front door sliding. She walks out of that room again, where I heard all those noises what feels like an eternity ago now.

Knowing she's back in the loft with me is comforting, and I calm down. She's still wearing the trench coat and heels, and that bag is still slung over her shoulder, though it looks heavier now. She's also carrying a small portable barbeque.

Strange...

There's more light coming through the windows, and I can see the details of her hair neatly thrown back in a ponytail, her face crisp, and just a few stitches around one eye. She probably went to a doctor. Some doctor that only works late in the night, where people like her do their business.

"Heather?"

She puts down the barbeque and the bag and takes out an aluminum can.

"Heather," I repeat louder, and she looks my way.

"What's behind that door?"

She starts pouring lighter fluid into the barbeque. "The answer to all your questions," she answers with a crooked smile, and then throws in a match. The flames shoot high before tempering down.

She spends another half hour preparing a new stage. Placing thick candles on tall sticks around the perimeter of the whipping bench, adjusting the lighting to where it's dark again except the flames that slowly tick up the temperature. *Dare I ask what's for dinner tonight?*

A faint yellow globe dangles overhead and the well-defined sounds of a classical orchestra emit from the speakers amidst a waft of lavender incense. It's a complete juxtaposition to what I worry may be in store for me. She moves the video camera closer. *She wouldn't hurt me now, would she?*

Something is not to her satisfaction because she rummages in her gigantic purse and then starts fussing over me again. She pulls my hair back, coating it with gel until it hardens in place, then secures it with an elastic band. "Did you ever take dance lessons?"

"Huh?" I tilt my head and squint my eyes.

She repeats the arbitrary question, but it's a welcome distraction.

I tell her it's not worth mentioning. That my mother took me to a ballet class once. I felt so much bigger and squatter than the other girls, and so much less coordinated. On top of having no rhythm. After class, the teacher suggested I try modern, and I'm sure she said a lot worse to my mother, because I was never pressured to go again.

"You have to know what someone's ready for before taking them to task." Her dexterous fingers settle loose wisps with bobby pins. "I used to follow the girls in school to their dance classes and watch them through the window." The bony fastener scrapes against my scalp. "What they were doing looked so…simple."

"I can attest to the fact that nothing about ballet was simple. Not for me, anyway."

"I bet you'd feel differently now." She presses her fingers along my lips and then digs in her purse again. "The color red was meant for lips like that."

The application of lipstick to my mouth reminds me of a time Janelle and I snuck into her mother's dressing room. It was filled with so much makeup and toiletries. My mother didn't have a tenth of that amount. Janelle pulled out a small gold-encased tube and told me she was going to make me even prettier. I could barely hold still as she applied the tacky paste evenly. I remember thinking she could've done whatever she wanted, as long as it meant I got to kiss her again.

Heather finally seems satisfied with her creation and drops her trench coat. Black, shiny latex hugs her curves like a cat woman suit and a huge, thick prosthetic penis is strapped to her hips. It's unnaturally big and my newly painted lips gape. *Is that for me?* Warmth spreads through my insides.

I've seen things like that before. I walked into one of *those* stores once after finding that video on the Internet that turned me on so much. I wanted to know if real people did things like that or if it was just for show. I was flustered when eventually the guy behind the counter asked if I needed help finding anything. I couldn't explain to him what I was looking for. I couldn't explain it to myself. I ran out of the place.

There's nowhere I can run to now.

She plucks one more item from her bag and gingerly places a black lace blindfold across my eyes. It obscures reality just enough to forget what those red coals could possibly be for, yet I can still see her every move.

"I want you to take it all," she says, running her palm up and down the length of her hefty rod. "And feel every sensation. Anticipation, fear, pleasure, pain…" It's like she's trying to coax an inanimate thing to life. "Don't focus on whether you can or should."

My insides flutter and the heat rises to my head, unsure whether I can handle all her kinks.

"Now open your mouth," she directs, rotating the black phallus up to the edge of my lips, pulling on the leather straps at my shoulders to coax me toward it.

I hesitate. I've never felt confident giving blow jobs, but this isn't...and she isn't...there I go analyzing everything again.

When I open my mouth, she shoves it in. Harder and deeper than I expected. Holding the sides of my face in place so I can't retract.

It feels brutal and barely fits in my mouth. I start choking and coughing, trying to breathe, spitting, wanting it out *now* when just moments ago, I wanted it in so much. But she keeps driving the rigid silicone deeper and deeper into my mouth, until my eyes well with tears. She reminds me that I need to let go of every hesitation in order to have it all.

I swear she's hell bent on having me hate her—or love her in the wrong kind of way. I try to calm my gag reflex by focusing on something different, like an anatomy class I took my first year in college, where we had to memorize the various parts of the throat. Epiglottis, larynx, pharynx. The words keep swimming through my mind until I almost vomit. Only then, when it's obvious that I've been pushed to another edge, does she take it out.

I gasp for breath like I've been underwater for too long. "Why did you do that?"

She grabs two candles and takes center stage. "When the goddess Artemis believed she was destined for a half-life because she'd sworn an oath to stay away from all men, the wiser and older Hestia had to show her more courageous ways to experience pleasure."

The recording light of the video camera catches my eye through the sheer blindfold. *Who is this extravagant show for this time?*

Licking the froth from around my mouth, I continue to watch her dance around in delicate, fluid fashion, wielding the candles like batons, her thick cock flapping between her thighs.

The strings begin their solo as she turns on a leg and gyrates the thing that nearly choked my sanity at my mouth again. "Maybe there's a better place for this."

Imagining her taking me with that thing that barely fit in my mouth makes my body throb even more fiercely this time. Especially when I feel it rub against that strap wedged between my cheeks like a chastity belt.

I push towards it, wishing her fingers to stop teasing and unhinge my sex—

No. Not my sex.

My pussy.

The chain attached to those clamps pulls hard. I let out a sharp exhale. My nipples are sore, but I yearn for more.

"You want it, don't you?" Her voice sounds magical amidst the rumble of percussion. "You want *me*, don't you?" She pulls at the restraints on my back and I feel the cinch around my breasts. It makes me pant.

I nod.

"Tell me what you want, Angie." I feel her hands at the buckle and her organ lying flaccid against my back. "You can't get what you want if you don't ask for it."

I don't want to tell her. I don't want to admit to all the thoughts that have been plaguing my mind, but my body is on an uncontrollable edge. "I want you."

Her fingers start to pull the strap out, but then stop. "You want me, or my big, juicy cock?"

The anticipation of feeling her inside me is unraveling what's left of my self-control. "I want...you." Inner thigh skin pinches against the robust latex. "And your...big, juicy cock." I can't believe the words are coming out of my mouth. "I want it all," I continue like a Stepford wife.

Satisfied with my admission, she pulls the last of the strap out and I feel it unhinge around my rear, the ache inside me growing more wild.

It's at the entrance to my pussy now, the head almost able to pop in, but not quite. I'm so wet. I move my hips, hoping to swallow it now the way I couldn't before, but she keeps teasing, until…with a grunt similar to a man's, she finally dives inside. I cry out, from her making me wait so long for the deliverance and from the size, filling me like nothing ever has.

The pungent smell of dried lilacs hangs thick in the air like storm clouds as I draw in a deep breath.

Her palms cup my bottom. "Once you get your mind past all its hang-ups, everything feels simple. Even ballet."

She takes me. At first gradually. As if this time, she wants to accustom me to the size, but then her thrusts become steadier and a tension builds on both sides of my pelvis.

My clitoris presses into the leather as my insides clench around her rod. Sweet nectar gushes like fruit candy from every intimate spot as she continues to pulse in and out, driving me closer to that release that is my only priority right now.

Suddenly she pulls out.

"No," I moan, feeling my body grind to an agonizing halt. "Please don't stop."

Beads of sweat line the creases of my mouth, and salty residue trickles onto my tongue. Her cock is so close. I know it is. So close to my…but not close enough.

"Please, put it back in. Please." My body bucks towards her, but she continues to pull away.

"Don't worry," she says in a provocative tone. "I'll put it back in. I'll even let you come."

The clamps around my nipples are pulled hard. I cry out.

"I know you want to come with me inside you." She leans her chest against my back, kneading my breasts, gripping my thighs.

I want her so badly.

"Every whore wants to come around a big, juicy cock," she says, nuzzling her mouth against my ear. And then she sits up. "All you have to do is admit what you are, and I'll put it back in." She runs her fingers slowly down the crack of my behind, stopping at my anus. It tightens. Her fingers continue down to my wetness, gently pinching the labia and rubbing all the sensitive folds, keeping my desire heightened.

My body swells with hunger and I feel out of my mind.

The thick latex is at my opening again. The head starts to stretch my circumference. "Come on, Angie, tell me what you are. Tell me you're a whore, so I can give you that release."

My mind fights with my body over the boundaries of pleasure, but I quickly learn that urgency will always win out over sensibility. "Whore," I say under my breath.

She inches into me, agonizingly slow, and then stops. "Who's a whore?"

"I am," I say in a trance. "I'm a whore."

She presses in, deeper and deeper, but tells me to keep saying it louder, or she won't let me have it all.

I do as she asks, yelling out that I'm a whore, not cognizant of its various shades of meaning as the temperature in the room continues to rise and that thick hardness fills me to the core.

My body clasps around it desperately until I finally feel the first waves of a climax roll into a thunderous orgasm that makes my body shake uncontrollably and my binds dig into me.

Her rhythm slows. I worry she's going to take it out again when my body wants more.

"I want you tell me when you're going to come again, Angie."

I feel a drop of wax against my skin. The unexpected shock of heat jolts me.

"If you tell me, I'm going to give you the type of pleasure that you will remember forever."

What she's proposing is unimaginable, but I'm delirious, so I nod, ready to tell her anything she wants to hear.

Sweat seeps from my every pore as the wax begins to drizzle... down the side of my neck, the round of my shoulder, into the bed of my arm, across my back and my lower cheeks. Every now and then, when it gets to be too much, I bellow out, but she responds only with the steady rhythm of her cock.

Incrementally, she works me into a frenzy. Dripping the wax until I can't register the heat anymore, plying her fingers through cooling textures, administering a noticeable spank whenever I try to get out of sync with her, shaping me into a masterpiece built on...courage.

We continue to move in unison for a long time. My body thrusting to meet hers, the leather slick under my responsive limbs and her hands taking turns being firm with every part of my body until I reach the brink of desire again.

If I'd never been told what sex was supposed to feel like, I'd hope this would be it. Anesthesia mixed with absurdity.

Something cold and metallic glides along my skin. I notice its stark contrast immediately, but it's too late for me to question or analyze my earlier trepidations. I cry out that I'm about to come as my body starts to buck and tug on its restraints.

As the words leave my mouth, I feel something scald my backside more distinctly than the hot wax. It takes my every sensation to new heights as the orgasm reverberates through my body. I wail at first, but she pushes inside me more fiercely, replacing the fear and pain with a numbing calm, helping me ride out every feeling and thought, until I collapse onto the leather.

Her thrusting stops and she pulls out.

Slowly, she unties the lace from across my eyes. Her fingers gently brush across my cheek. I feel her lips at my ear. "Who's the whore now?" she whispers.

I hear the clang of something fall to the ground.

TWELVE

I'm sitting across from her in the claw-foot tub. The water is steaming, almost flowing over the lip, and I'm sweating. The type of sweat you get not just from the temperature being too hot but from your mind going a bit mad.

The collar around my neck feels tight, and the chains between my collar and the cuff around each wrist feel short. I need to get out of here. I'm not doing enough. I'm letting her unravel me by tapping into a part of my sexuality that I've always been curious about, but it's not right. It shouldn't be happening like this.

I don't want to learn everything about myself under duress and in such a condensed period of time. If this was a normal relationship, we could get comfortable with one another at every new stage, first. I know she could teach me a lot. Behind the crazy façade is someone obviously strong, independent, confident, and street-smart. I've never had any of that. But a normal relationship with her seems preposterous.

I raise the beer she's given me to my lips and hear the part of the chain that's wrapped around an exposed pipe at the wall softly clink against the white porcelain of the tub. The cold beer feels good sliding down my hot insides.

Her eyelids droop, and she leans her head back as if she's about to fall asleep. Without all the makeup, her cuts and bruises are more visible. She looks like she's been brawling in some alley. But it only gives her more character. The empty beer bottle drops from her hand and echoes up the tall walls of the bathroom. Her legs fall leisurely into mine. I press my legs closer.

"Are your parents still together?" she asks, running the water through her fingers.

I nod.

"In love?" Sarcasm laces her voice.

I shrug.

My parents are really more like good friends. They spend a lot of time together, except at night, when they resign to separate bedrooms. I once asked my mom about it and she told me that couples who sleep together are more likely to divorce. When I started seeing Erik and having sex with him on a regular basis, I wondered what my parents' sex life was like. *Did they even have sex anymore?* I couldn't imagine having sex with Erik and then getting up to go to a separate room, but I never asked her about all that.

"My dad left when I was thirteen," Heather confides, and then reaches for the latch of the mini-fridge she's situated next to the tub. Her hands struggle to open the fresh beer. I almost offer to help, but then she manages like always to get the job done.

"Ugly fights, ugly divorce." She makes a fist and punches the air as if reliving the past. "But then his younger brother, Uncle Johnny, started hanging around." Her mouth curls into a smile. "He was very attractive and very nice, and Mom sure did like having him at the house." Her lips linger around the tip of the beer bottle. "He'd come over every Sunday after church. Fix stuff while Mom made

dinner. And then after dinner, after they were sure I was asleep…
he'd fix her up too." She starts laughing. "The way she wailed and
the way he grunted, it was almost as bad as the fights Mom and
Dad used to have. But she let him come back every Sunday. He
must've been doing something right."

She taps the side of the tub. "And you know what's crazy?"

I peel the label from my beer bottle. "What?"

"It started turning me on." She takes a big gulp. "Yup. My
lower regions would ache so much, I started touching myself to
get some relief—but it only made it worse. Until one time, I snuck
downstairs and saw what they were doing." Her eyes glaze over
as if the moment is imprinted forever in her mind. "I realized I
wanted Uncle Johnny to do the same thing to me that he was doing
to Mom."

What she's saying makes me uneasy. I've never had thoughts
like *that*, and I've felt embarrassed about the ones I consider most
impure. Like the ones about Janelle. And that video on the Internet.

"What happened?" I ask, even though I'm not sure I want to
know.

"I started putting on makeup, like my mom, and wearing
dresses on Sunday, when I knew he'd be around. Eventually he
started looking at me…differently."

"Didn't your mom notice?"

"That I was turning into a woman? I'm sure. I'd just turned
fourteen, I'm sure she thought it was normal."

She places the sweating beer bottle on her neck. "One day I
left school early, because my stomach was cramping. He drove up
as I was walking home and offered me a ride. Mom was still at
work when we got there. I went to my room and laid down on the

bed, and the cramps got real bad, so I called out for him. When he walked in, I was a mess. Thrashing around, my dress hiked above my waist, trying to knock out the pain."

She pauses to take another sip of her beer. I can't tell whether the memory is going to make her cry...or smile.

"He got me some aspirin and water at first, but then he stood there, not saying anything. He had this look in his eye. And then I felt him on top of me. Pinned my hands, parted my thighs, ripped my panties off, and stifled my screams with his other hand. And then I felt him, his hardness, pushing its way inside of me, and I started kicking and trying to fight him off, but he kept tearing and digging into something deep inside me, making those same noises I'd heard him make with Mom. And when it was over, he told me to clean up. Told me I'd just gotten my period and that I would be alright."

"He raped you," I say harshly, letting pieces of the beer label fall into the water.

She slaps the water and snickers when my eyes blink from the irritation, as if the accusation is far too serious for the crime. "It was just like I'd always fantasized."

She's delusional. "You were fourteen. You were trying to fight him off."

The muscles of her inner thighs contract around me. "I didn't want to disappoint him. I was only doing what I saw my mom do... because I wanted him to come back."

I finish what's left of my beer. "Did he?"

"Every Wednesday, for almost two years." She slides her free hand up her chest. Her fingers linger on her collarbone and then wrap around her throat. "Until Mom got a new boyfriend."

I slide as far back against the tub as I can. It irritates the sore spot on my rear where she marked me with the iron brand. "Why did you tell me that? Am I supposed to feel sorry for you?"

She lets out a chuckle. "Just a little girl talk, Angie. You know, getting to know one another better. Stop being so uptight."

I feel her foot try to wriggle its way between my calves.

"I think we've gotten to know one another as much as I ever want to."

She places her beer on top of the mini-fridge and moves closer to me, spreading my legs apart. "Oh yeah, what else do you think?"

"That *this* has gone as far as it's going to go." I grab the edge of the tub, trying to stabilize myself, but there's not enough slack between the chains around my wrists, and I almost drop my beer bottle. "That you're never going to get any more than *this* out of me."

She grasps my thighs and her eyes open wide. "And what's *'this,'* Angie?"

Her fingers dig into me, awakening that part of me that didn't exist before this last weekend. It makes me flush. "I don't know... sex...carnal lust...physical chemistry."

She smiles, as if my admission has vindicated her. "Really? And what else?"

"That if you were raped by your uncle and enjoyed it, it goes a long way to explaining...what happened with that city inspector."

She lets go and pushes off me.

"You think everything's so black and white." She props herself up on her knees, sitting up tall. She looks statuesque. The moonlight is hitting the water on her skin just right, making it glisten. I can't believe this beautiful woman has the potential to turn so ugly on the flip of a dime.

I grip my dangling beer bottle harder.

"That everything we want is so simple," she continues, "and everything dark we naturally reject."

I move my gaze to the chain and key dangling between her breasts.

"I told you that story, not because I wanted a chiding or your pity." Her fingers move up each of my legs. "I told you that story because it's about choices. I chose to let him do what he did to me. Even if some would call it wrong."

Her fingers continue playing, getting closer to my most sensitive parts. My breathing hastens under her spell.

"For example, what if I told you that the front door was open right now."

I grip my bottle.

"What would you do?"

The front door feels so far away, and I'm chained to a wall…it's hopeless. Unless I kicked her, and broke the bottle, and pulled hard enough on the pipe I'm chained to…

She starts to gently tease my pussy and my hips rise, uncontrollably, distracting my thoughts. *What is wrong with me?!*

"And even if it were locked, the key is right here in front of you." She leans over me and the key knocks into my face. "You could grab it again and bolt."

One of her fingers slips inside of me and I let out a gasp. She bites at my ear, then cheek, and my mouth turns to hers. Her tongue circles my lips, her relentless nature drawing me in.

Her fingers glide up my taint and circle my rosebud. *This is exactly like that video that turned me on so much…but also like that awkward experience with Erik.*

We were fooling around naked and started doing it. I'd just seen the video. After a while, I pulled it out and started pushing it in somewhere else. He was apprehensive. Kept asking if I was sure. I didn't want to analyze it. I just wanted to do it.

I tense up. The way I did when I sensed Erik's uncertainty, and my sudden reluctance is noticeable.

She nudges her lips against mine, kissing me tenderly. As her tongue slithers further into my mouth so does the tip of her finger into that spot...

"Have you ever done it this way?" she asks, running her lips along my ear as her other hand wanders down my arm.

I tell her I haven't, because I eventually told Erik to stop. It didn't feel right. Not like what I'd expected. I could tell he felt bad, even though it had been my idea. He held me and told me not to worry about it. That he wasn't into that kind of kinky shit anyway and that I shouldn't feel pressured. That he was totally happy with our sex life.

He didn't understand that I wasn't.

"But you've always wanted to." Her fingers move back to my throbbing slit and hasten their pace.

How does she know that? I swim into her, reveling in the salty tastes of her mouth and the idea of acting out my dirtiest fantasy... with her.

She feels my grip around the bottle and her thumb deftly lands on my clit. My hips rock and I'm completely helpless.

I release the bottle.

When it lands with a loud clang on the tile, she grabs the back of my head and kisses me harder. My body quivers and she pulls my hips under hers.

The water sloshes under my chin and we're completely entangled in one another. I feel the now familiar edge of a climax coming on...but then she drives my head under the water and forcefully keeps it down.

I open my mouth to scream and quickly realize I need to stop. Water rushes into my lungs. I kick and thrash, but she's got me completely pinned. I swallow more water and my head starts to feel heavy...

She yanks me up by my hair.

I cough, spit, and desperately inhale. I can't believe I let her... that I wanted her...again. Blood rushes furiously through my veins and I lunge at her, only to have the collar slingshot me back.

I hit the porcelain hard.

"I hate you!" I scream at her and kick as hard as I can.

The water splashes around us as I try to rip myself from the pipe in the wall, landing a few good kicks to the side of her thighs. *I should have never let go of that bottle,* I scold myself.

She leaps out of the tub and I try to clamber after her, but manage only to scrape my elbows and knees.

She grabs a remote sitting next to the sink. She presses play and turns on the television hanging on the wall in front of the tub.

I see myself from the night before. Stretched out, pinned down, and her, taking me. I turn away, humiliated by what I've let her do to me.

"I chose," she says, trying to catch her breath. She fast-forwards the video until I hear myself yelling out, about all the things I want her to do to me, and about the whore that I am.

She grabs my chin and forces me to look at the TV screen. "You don't hate me. You chose to let me do that to you because it gave you something you needed."

The video continues to play.

I watch myself giving in to her, being branded by her. My most impure thoughts exposed for everyone to see.

THIRTEEN

She's gone. So is everything else. The workbench and all the tools, the whipping horse, the cameras, even the mini-fridge that she wedged into the bathroom last night. Gone.

The loft is back to its sparse condition. I walk over to the kitchen and look at what she's left out for me. Toast, butter, jam, a glass of orange juice, and a fresh tank top and underwear. I check the size on both. Medium. I don't fit into Medium. I've always been a Large.

I let the sheet around me drop to the floor and try on the clean attire. It hugs, but not tightly, which surprises me.

Next to the plate there's a note. On it she's written: *I'll be home by 6:00 p.m.* I look up at the clock. It's just before eleven in the morning. I pick up the plastic knife and slowly butter the bread, and then add a thin layer of jam. I take a bite, but quickly set the bread back on the paper plate.

I've always wanted to lose weight. I scold myself for the proposition. *How can I worry about that right now?* It's as ridiculous as when I bought a month's worth of laxatives in eleventh grade. It's probably a good thing my mother found them before I got through even half.

I pick up the plastic cup of juice instead. It's room temperature and overly sweet, but I gulp it down anyway. Juice dribbles down my chin, staining my new tank top. *Figures.* I walk to the faucet and turn it on, trying to blot out the yellow.

I look around for a dishtowel and notice the charging unit next to the door—except the stun gun is not there. I look at the plastic utensils, then back over at the supply of electricity.

Of course.

I grab the knife and fork and run over to the bed, crawling under it towards the wall with the crack in the floorboard, hoping my cell phone is still there.

I peer down.

It's still there.

I carefully lower the utensils into the crack. They give me just the extra leverage I need to touch the cell phone. I scoop the fork under the phone and start lifting it…but it falls. I try various arrangements with the utensils, but the phone continues to slip.

Finally I manage to prop the phone up on its side, where the plug-in resides for a headset. I jam one of the fork tines into the hole and it sticks. Carefully, I start lifting it again, with the knife under the phone for extra stability.

It's out.

I wail with joy, overly ecstatic for the small victory. I roll out from under the bed, clasping the phone, and jump up and down, until my momentary elation dissipates.

Does my phone even matter anymore?

With Erik potentially in the midst of some new affair, is he even going to care about my text messages? Will I be able to reach *anyone* who cares?

I shake off the negative thoughts. I haven't been so innocent the last few days either. I left with a stranger when he didn't show up. Maybe he latched on to someone else because he hasn't been able to get a hold of me. The truth may be a lot more complicated than Heather is making it out to be.

I run back over to where the stun gun usually charges and examine how to possibly get the unit to power my phone. I hold my phone to the probes in different ways, but no dice.

I realize I need a conductor. Something metal, a wire of some sort that will allow the electricity to pass. But I know she doesn't have that kind of stuff lying around.

I wander, contemplating, but end up looking in all the same places I did several days ago and don't find anything different.

A heavy thud resonates through the loft.

My heart pounds in my chest. Her note said she wouldn't be home until six. I look at the clock above the cabinet again. It's only twenty past eleven.

Has the clock stopped working?

The noises continue. I look down at the phone I'm holding. I need to hide it. I make my way back towards the bed and stick the phone between the mattress and the box spring. I kick the plastic cutlery I used out of view.

The bumping sounds are coming from behind that same door…

Every step I take gives my mind more reason to race with awful scenarios. *This is where the crazy city inspector lives. This is where she's hiding all the dead bodies.* Or maybe someone received my cries for help and found where I was at…except she got to them first.

What if she got to Erik first?

Palms sweating, I put my ear to the door and listen. Something is definitely in there. I reach for the doorknob, wondering how I'll open it if it's locked and whether I can just bust through the door. Maybe I should turn around.

I continue to stare at the door. *Didn't curiosity kill the cat?*

Heart racing, I turn the knob. To my surprise, it opens. And nothing jumps out. I peer carefully inside. The adrenaline is flowing through my veins so hard, my limbs are quaking, but I continue my quest.

It's pungent, like the air hasn't moved through here in weeks. And it's pitch black—almost. I spot a barely noticeable red blinking light at the very back above another door. She's recording *all* of this. She left the door open on purpose. I should turn back. *No.* I can't let her intimidate me. If I'm ever going to get out of here, she has to know I won't just curl up and…I don't want to think about that possibility right now.

I run my hand up the side of the wall, hoping to find a light switch. No luck. I take another step in and hear light shuffling, like a parade of rats running across a dusty floor. It's unnerving and makes me wish I was wearing some kind of footwear…but I can't turn around now.

I wave my hand in front of me and feel a string. I tug on it and a dim bulb illuminates the room.

My gaze falls on something that I've only ever seen in textbooks and photos my parents have developed. It's an Iron Maiden. I'm in awe that she would actually have something like this.

The medieval artifact rests upright, and I walk closer to it, careful not to step on any of the broken debris and glass scattered over the floor.

Its shell is ornately embossed and an Aztec-like head adorns the top. A crank handle latches it together, and it appears to be attached to a wooden frame on the wall—although part of the frame is broken off and lying on the concrete floor. That must have been the loud bang I heard initially.

I run my hand over the crank handle and discover a keyhole. The bumping noises start up again along with a dull whimpering, like the one I first heard days ago. Someone is definitely in there.

"Hold on!" I yell, sweat dripping into my eyes. "I'm going to help you!" I pull the handle in every direction before realizing it's not in my power to force it open. I have to find the key that opens this capsule. I step back and start looking around.

To my right is that other door. I pull hard on its knob, but it's locked. To my left is some old dusty shelving with even older-looking decanters, bottles of wine, cans of vegetables, boxes of crackers. Probably the reason for the stifling smell in here. I peer closer. It's like something you would see on a survivalist show. Except for the bottles of hydrochloric acid, which bring disturbing thoughts.

Something runs across my feet and I scream, jumping back so far, I hit the wall. From this vantage, I see a handful of cockroaches in the corner that have congregated around what looks to be a ring of keys and some roach traps. I squat down and swat the large insects away from the carcasses before carefully picking up what could be exactly what I'm looking for.

I try each key on the ring, hoping to find one that fits. The cries from inside get louder until finally I hear a click.

The lock opens. I take a deep breath, grab the crank handle again, and turn it.

The door swings open and the wild eyes of a woman with long blonde hair meet mine. She's gagged and tied into the Iron Maiden. One wide leather strap stretches across her midsection, fastening her arms tightly to each side. Another strap is over her shoulders, and another one holds her legs in place. She's wearing a short, tight black dress, like something you'd wear to a nightclub. Her makeup is smeared, like she hasn't washed her face in a long while.

"Oh my god." The words barely escape my mouth. I'm too abhorred by thoughts of how she ended up here. My hands shake even harder as I reach up to remove her gag. "Are you alright?"

The woman starts sniveling. "I need to get out!" she yells, struggling against the leather bonds.

"Okay, okay, let me help you." I grab the strap around her shoulders, but her struggling makes it difficult to get enough leverage to pull it apart. "If you just hold on, I think I can undo this."

"Get if off, get it off! Get me out of here!" She continues to thrash.

I try to hold her still, but she's making everything impossible.

I finally stop and put my hands around her face. "You need to calm down."

Our eyes fix on one another and I'm able to take a good look at her. She's so familiar, but I can't quite place why…

"Calm down, and I know I'll be able to get you out of here."

I grab the top buckle again, push her back a little, and start pulling on the strap. It takes a few tries, but the strap finally gives. I do the same with the one around her waist, and as this one loosens, the blonde falls forward onto me, off-balance and unable to support her own weight.

We're both panting, and I put my arms around her to try and comfort her. "How long have you been in here?"

"I don't know," she sobs. "I lost…I lost track. What day is it?"

I have to think about it. I've also lost track of time. "Tuesday, I think."

Her sobs become more intense. "Wha…what m…mo…month?"

I tell her it's August. Waves of anguish engulf her and she spasms in my arms. I hold on to her tighter. "What's your name?"

"R-ach-rach-el," she manages to stutter.

"Rachel, I'm Angie, and I'm going to get you out of here." I carefully push her up and out of my arms. "I'm going to get us both out of here." I suddenly feel an intense resolution to help this girl and myself break free from this cage. I don't know what I've been thinking the last few days. Immersed in some sexual self-discovery. Blinded by Heather's stories. Empathizing with a woman who's capable of doing *this* and much worse. I'll never be able to trust her. I can't believe I had thoughts of what a relationship would be like with her. *What kind of a foundation would it be built on, mind games and deceit?*

Rachel braces herself as I start working on the buckle around her ankles. It releases with more ease.

"You have to hurry…she'll be back any moment," Rachel says in a desperate voice.

"No, she wrote a note that said she wouldn't be back 'til six. We have time." I help Rachel step out of the Iron Maiden, holding her up with my arms.

The steps we take are agonizing and slow. Rachel is weak and it's hard for me to hold up a tall girl. But eventually I'm able to sit her down on the couch. She tells me she's thirsty, so I quickly walk to the kitchen to get her some water.

When I hand her the plastic cup, she gulps down the liquid

fiercely. She holds it out to me again, signaling for more, and I run to refill it. On my way back, I grab my leftover toast and hand that to her as well.

She devours the toast and starts gulping more water. It settles her down a bit. "How are you going to get us out of here?" She's incredulous.

I sit down next to her not knowing exactly how to answer her question. "I…I've been trying to find a way to charge my cell phone."

A few remaining crumbs line her mouth and she wipes them with her forearm, observing me like a thoroughbred at the races.

Finally, she throws the plastic plate to the floor. "You don't know how to get us out of here?!" she screams, ready to throw a tantrum.

I shift away from her.

"I was *safe* in there!" She beats the sofa with her palms. "Do you know what she'll do if she finds me out here, like this?!"

"You were trapped, not safe," I correct the frantic woman next to me.

She grits her teeth. "She told me she'd love me as long as I did everything I was told."

My head shakes in disagreement of everything that statement implies.

"Why would you want her love?" By the state of Rachel's clothes and the stench coming off her body, I wouldn't be surprised if she's been locked in that Iron Maiden since May and has lost her mind.

"She takes care of me."

I spot a tear near the bottom of her dress. I place my hand gently over top, wanting to fix it. "How did you end up in there?"

She doesn't answer and instead tells me she needs to use the bathroom. I point to it and she tries to stand, but doesn't quite have her balance, so I put my arm under her again and take her there.

She lets go of me and hikes up her dress, stumbling towards the toilet in her tall platform heels.

I turn around to give her privacy.

"I like this tub," I hear her say, completely calm, as she urinates. "It's been a long time since I've been in it."

I lean against the doorway. "You've been in that tub before?"

The toilet flushes and the water runs, and then I feel her bony hand on my shoulder. "Cell phones don't work too well in here."

Goose bumps form on my arms. Her omen is chilling.

She walks past me and I sit down next to her again on the couch. *Why does she look so familiar?*

"How do you know Heather?" I ask.

"We met at a club." She tugs at her dress. Her bony elbows look like they might pierce through her skin. "How 'bout you?"

I squeeze the cushion of the sofa. "A club called Beso?"

She nods.

I look to the wall with all the portraits and think back to the pictures I found in the darkroom.

She's the girl.

I look at her carefully again...it's eerie looking at someone you thought had suffered an irreversible fate.

"Look, there are two of us. We can fight her off—"

"Fight her off?" Rachel laughs sardonically. "You can't. And if you think you can..." She gets in my face and then one of her fingers grazes my jaw line. "What is it about you that she likes more...?"

"I don't understand."

She sniffs at me like a dog sniffs an animal to get more cues on what's distinctive. "I don't have the same options as you."

Her words still don't resonate with me. "I heard you trying to get out. You told me you wanted to get out of here."

A twisted smile forms on her face. "I was just letting her know I was hungry and needed to use the bathroom." She holds out her rail-thin wrists to me. "Understand?"

I look down at her wrists. They have the same cuff marks as mine, but also the marks of someone having taken a razor to them. I notice her badly chipped nail polish and her dried-out, grown out, platinum dye job. Her mousy features, pretty upon first glance, are too pointy to ever be beautiful.

I take her hands and pull her up to stand. She's taller, but only because of the grubby platform heels she's wearing, and everything droops on her, including that awful polyester dress, because she's too thin and has no curves.

I think for the first time in my life, I do understand. I'm out here for a reason. Heather locked *her* away—not me. She could've killed me by now and she hasn't. Maybe she never intends to. I don't want to jeopardize that. Rachel is right. We can't outfight her. There's a better way to get out of here than that.

I lead Rachel back to the Iron Maiden, cautious not to compromise her fragile state. *Wouldn't want Heather to start liking me any less…*

She steps into it and I put all the ties and leather straps back in place. When I'm done, I look up at the red light and smirk, before reaching for the lid. I look at Rachel one more time. She looks… comfortable.

I swing the lid shut.

FOURTEEN

I've removed any evidence of ever making contact with Rachel. I've also decided I'm not going to confront Heather about what happened, because she probably knows...and knows that *I know* she knows. She left that door open to test my loyalty. And I have a feeling I made the right decision.

The big hand on the clock in the kitchen nears the number three and I find myself fidgeting with a new awareness. This entire time I've been looking at my circumstances from the perspective of a victim and an outsider, because Heather's so much more physical and sexual and experienced than me. I'll never be able to compete with that. But the layers are much more complex beneath our skin. The epidermis alone has five strata.

She doesn't want someone exactly like her anyway. She wants someone to challenge *her* status quo. Not physically outpower her, or succumb to her every fancy, but take her emotions by surprise. It hadn't occurred to me, until now, that my best shot at getting out of here may be to give *her* something that *she* needs.

It will intimidate her. And intimidating a predator, even via bluffing, can be an efficient means of defense for prey. There's a well-known experiment between the peacock butterfly and the Blue Paridae bird that proves exactly that. The butterfly, instead of wavering in the wake of its predator, beats its wings and hisses. The bird, having the impression of a much mightier opponent, gives up its advances and moves on to an easier target.

The doorway to Heather's dressing room feels like I'm on the precipice of a major commitment. *Can I really make her believe that I've fallen in love with her? Will it be enough to make her fall in love with me?*

I walk toward the plastic bins and open some of them. I thumb through the racks. She's got everything from extravagant gowns you'd see on the Oscars red carpet to business attire…and all those costumes. This world of playing dress-up and putting on a façade is so foreign to me, yet it reminds me in some ways of my time with Janelle. She was so unpredictable and would always push me to do things I wouldn't have ever thought to do on my own. Like sneak out of her house during our last sleepover before she moved and skinny dip in the pool three doors down. I was so scared, but the rush gave me such a high. And once we were in the pool, laughing, playing, getting as close as we'd ever come…it was the bravest I'd ever been.

Until now.

A bin towards the very back is filled with lingerie. Some is made of leather, some has lace, some is silky, some rubbery. I've only bought lingerie once. It was for Erik's graduation. I felt so fat in the dressing room and the salesgirl kept bringing me stuff that only made me feel fatter. Finally I told her to bring me the most basic black strapless bra, and underwear that covered as much of my butt as possible.

Despite all my self-conscious thoughts, Erik ravished me that night. It was the closest I'd ever come to having an orgasm with a man.

I start picking through what she has and wonder if falling in love with her is such a farfetched notion. I'm attracted to her, and no one has ever gotten me this hot. She consumes my most subconscious thoughts and even when I know I should hate her, I still yearn for her touch. But she's crazy and frightening, so I know this is purely a blundering lust. I have to be careful not to lose myself in it. Put up an emotional wall if I feel myself slipping, like I had to after I crashed my dad's car.

A year after Janelle left town, I took a turn too fast on Sunset. The back end spun and eventually hit a tree. Luckily there were no witnesses, so I couldn't be charged with reckless driving and the insurance company covered all the costs. It was an accident. I'd never been an assertive driver, my mother said. For once, I wanted everyone to believe that. Not question why my grades were slipping or why I was eating so much…more, and why I barely left the house.

I search more aggressively, as if finding the right piece will bring me one step closer to figuring everything out. I grab a few things that look to be closest to my size and head to her bathroom.

I examine myself in the full-length mirror hung on the back of the door, catching a glimpse of the claw-foot tub. I can't believe that she opened up to me about all that personal stuff *and* tried to drown me in that tub. *Or did she?* It's all so confusing.

I take off my tank top and underwear.

I've always hated doing this. Getting naked in any light. But today my stomach doesn't slope out as much, and my thighs look more firm than full of cellulite, and my breasts appear more defined. I slowly turn around, analyzing every angle, and for the first time, I don't dislike what I see.

The WHORE mark she branded on my behind is still raw to the touch. I think of the meltdown I had when I first saw it. I wanted to punch her lights out. And she just stood back, shaking her head, amused by my anger, as if there was something I wasn't willing to understand.

I run my fingers over the letters now, thinking about how many women before me have been labeled with this title. Not streetwalkers hooked on smack, but women who were confident in who they were and weren't ashamed to say and do whatever they wanted.

That's what she was trying to get across to me.

I squat down and hold up my favorite of the things I've picked out. It's this black vinyl two-piece number. The bottoms are so tight, I can barely stretch them over my calves and thighs. They sit below my hip bones, ensuring that when I bend over, nearly everything will spill out. They also have appropriately placed holes at every private part. I like that.

The top is a very low-cut vest. It lifts my breasts up and out so they look bigger than ever. For once, this doesn't bother me. I slide into a pair of black patent peep-toe platform heels and practice my walk towards and away from the mirror. The more I do it, the more stable I become. Taking my time to walk in the heels also alters my posture. I suck in my stomach and straighten my shoulders. It makes my butt and chest stick out. Everything looks so perky and well-defined.

I reach for the long, sleek black wig I find in a different bin and walk to her bathroom sink to find something to secure it with.

Wedged between all those bottles of pills is a slice of cardboard holding plastic bobby pins. I tuck my hair to make the wig sit better. The dark hair gives my light features a nice contrast.

Her makeup bag rests on top of the toilet, and I reach for it hesitantly. *My mother rarely wears makeup,* I muse, as I pluck at my skin, assessing where to start. She's naturally beautiful though, with her large, deep-set black eyes and lashes so long…other women have to pay for lashes like that. Her lips are perfectly plump and her cheekbones are high. Her nose, though a little large, gives her character.

Me, on the other hand, I inherited more of my dad's Irish features. The freckles, light eyes and brows, and the round face. Luckily, I got my mom's plump lips. People always comment on how nice my lips are.

I take out the foundation and start applying like I imagine one should. Like Janelle taught me once.

I wipe away the dark circles and other imperfections until my skin looks Photoshopped. I layer some black eyeliner and shadows, ranging from brown to cream, on my lids and then heavily work in mascara on the top and bottom of each eye. I manage to find appropriate rouge and lipstick for my cheeks and lips, and top it off by dabbing some Chanel No. 5 on my neck that I find in a small flask in a side pocket of her makeup bag.

When I assess the finished product in the mirror, I barely recognize what was there before. I look older, less innocent, like a horny housewife about to unleash on the unsuspecting husband who's had a long day. The only thing missing is a martini in hand. I let out a laugh. Martinis are for people who lack conviction.

I strut out of the bathroom and towards the bed, and sit down, playing with different poses. I imagine Erik walking in, wearing the tux he wore graduation night, and lean to my side. He looked so slick, not just like some jock in sweaty gym clothes and a lazy five o'clock shadow. His broad shoulders and tight butt filled everything out just right. He looked like a man, and the way he looked at me… like I was a woman to contend with.

"You want this?" I say to him, pretending to run my hands down the plush velvet of the Jessica Rabbit dress I wore that night. The fabric hugs me tightly, propping me up to be bold. He laughs a little uncomfortably, as if my proposition is making him shy for the first time. When he gets within arm's reach, I shake my finger at him and take one last sip from my glass of champagne.

"No, no, you're going to have to show me you deserve it first," I say, before pushing him down into his desk chair. His mouth opens slightly because he wants to be funny. He's not used to this type of tension between us. I don't let him go there. Instead I kiss him. Not a young, wet kiss, but a deep, lascivious one.

The camera on his laptop is turned on and I can see us, mouths engrossed, in a small window of the screen. I make it bigger and then snap a photo. His hands wander between the long slit and firmly grip the tops of my thighs. He asks what I'm doing. I don't know, I tell him. Maybe it's something I've always wanted to do. Maybe it's the glass of champagne I've just had. The light seems right, and we look good right now. This is how it should be always. I set the timer to continue snapping every five seconds and then I spin the chair around and arch my back over his desk, ready for him to take me, ready for it to feel different this time. I start making all those noises you make when you're just about to climax.

I decide to wait for Heather like this, wondering if I have the courage to command her like that.

FIFTEEN

The door slides open. Heather pauses in surprise.

"Have something on your mind?" Her voice is uncertain as she walks in my direction.

"I've done some thinking," I say, propping up on my elbows. I curl my fingers through the tips of my new dark hair. "I'm not sure when I'm getting out of here, so why continue to waste time?"

She towers over me and crosses her arms. One hip juts out to the side, like she won't be convinced until she hears more.

I pull at my leggings and hike my cleavage, fighting any trepidations. It might be better if I stand up.

In my platform heels I'm almost able to meet her wary glance. "Maybe I need to embrace a different destiny."

She sighs in disbelief.

I place my hands on her defensive stance and kiss her gently. She doesn't respond. It's as if my mouth—the mouth she's been craving for nearly a week—is suddenly unremarkable to her. I understand. She's expecting loathing and having to manipulate me into doing the things she wants.

I can't let that stop me.

I dive in again, this time more forcefully, weaving my hands through her hair, making noises similar to those I was practicing on the bed. "Heather, I want to give you pleasure. The way you've given me pleasure," I whisper in her ear.

"You've accused me of getting you drunk, coercing you. Just last night you hated me. Strong words for someone who now wants to bring me pleasure."

I glide my hands along the satin of her jacket. "I knew what I wanted from the moment I saw you on the dance floor."

She stops my hands midway down her arm and squeezes them. Hard. Reminding me of who's in charge. "What do you know about giving a woman pleasure?"

"I may not know all the fancy tricks you do, but I know a genuine smile and the subtle gestures of permission." I break free of her grasp and intertwine my fingers between hers. "The bow of a head, flutter of lashes, relaxing of shoulders, allowing me to try…"

Hesitantly, she drops her arms, giving me an opening.

I guide her jacket off and let it fall to the floor, not allowing our gaze to break, and then smack my lips against hers, drinking greedily from her mouth.

She breaks away to once again inspect. "What if this is just a temporary trick of the light? Something different to distract me."

My hands wrap around her waist and slowly untuck her blouse. "Didn't you tell me that different was good?"

The rouge begins to smear between our cheeks.

I unbutton the few buttons of her light blouse and pull it off her arms.

Her fingers glide along the edge of my leggings. I suck in my stomach more.

"Careful, Angie. I like you like this."

I smile. *It's working.* The blouse slips through my fingers like the last rays of light before sunset. I tug at her to follow me back to the bed.

This is it. My nerves are a mess. The rush of my power play is catching up to me.

I push her down under me and, as if we were starved for too long, nails dig into flesh and drag down backs, wanting to pierce skin. Eyes drip with desire. Heartbeats pound loudly over the slight creak of mattress underneath.

The magnetism between us grows and even though this was a precisely calculated move on my part, I allow it to take over. Unzipping her pencil skirt and pulling hard to get it over her sculpted behind and thighs. Her eyes have a bright and youthful spark. She bends her knees, ready for me.

I put a tight grip over her smooth underwear and massage my palm over her mound, a bit nervous about whether I'll be able to perform to her satisfaction. So many ways to begin. I've imagined them all, even when I didn't want to. Her midsection rises, beckoning me to start.

I crawl onto her, breathing heavily over her lace-covered breasts, flicking my tongue at what's underneath. I'm in control. We're both aroused by that.

I unclasp her bra and bring my lips to one of her meaty nipples, sucking, making it bigger. *God, I could suck on it forever.* I know it's driving her crazy. I can tell because her hips grind against my thigh.

My mouth circles around it, biting down on it every now and then, and she moans like an animal in heat. I slide one of my hands into the tight pinch of her underwear and let one of my fingers explore between her folds. The warm sponginess is familiar, yet different. I revel in discovering that I can make her as wet as she makes me and how different strokes with my fingers on different parts of her vulva put her into varying states of roused panic.

When I find her clitoris, I note how it feels similar to mine. No bigger than the tip of my pinky finger. I rub over and around it. Like I've done to myself before. Like she's done to me. It gets harder and harder, just like mine does.

I slide into her warm insides.

I can tell by the noises she's making and the way her body is reacting that I'm doing something right. I keep my finger lightly pulsing and use my thumb to circle her sensitive nub until I find a pace that I sense is just right. I keep rubbing and sinking my finger until she convulses around me and suddenly, liquid seeps over my hand.

Wow. I just gave her an orgasm.

It feels completely different from giving a man an orgasm. It's more subdued and eloquent. Or maybe she's just that refined.

I stop sucking on her nipple and look up. She's spent. Her eyes are closed, her mouth is slightly ajar, and her breathing is quieting. She doesn't look like a beast on a war path anymore, only beautiful, like the night we met. It reminds me of why I was attracted to her in the first place, why I let her take me home with her, and why I allowed myself to delve into something…different. I know it was my frustration with Erik and the alcohol to an extent, and I know I blamed it on that the next day, but there was also something about her. She was the yin to my yang and I'd only ever felt that once before.

Remembering the camera in the drawer of the end table, I reach for the latch and open it quietly, not wanting to wake her. The camera is still there, but all the receipts have been removed… it's not important right now.

I focus the zoom on the perfect arch of her one eyebrow and click the shutter button. Flecks of mascara have amassed under each eye and I document this next because it gives the impression of a woman who's worked too hard to notice. The lens moves down to the dark mole near her rib cage, and every time the aperture opens and closes, I've caught another detail of the woman preoccupying my mind.

If only things hadn't gotten so ugly and complicated, and so quickly. I turn on the lamp to get a softer hue. After testing the focus about an arm's length from where she lies, I slide back down next to her, nuzzling my face into her neck and inhaling her musty scent. Maybe she could've been my…I scold myself for so quickly losing sight of my mission. I'm supposed to make *her* fall in love with me, not the other way around.

I run my fingers along the black lace of her bra and untwist one of the straps. I lift the camera back to where I tested the focus. Pictures begin to snap of two women in bed. Their eyes are closed. Maybe they're sleeping, or maybe they're enjoying a brief moment that's out of the ordinary for both of them. They could be a couple, strictly lovers, or considering a change to the status quo.

The camera lets out a mechanical whirl, signaling the film's end. I lower the camera, enjoying the stillness of the moment, listening to our shallow breaths syncopate in an irregular pattern.

"Impressive." She yawns and stretches. "Not many people can use that piece so deftly."

Her voice startles me. I thought she was in a deep sleep. "Something I picked up."

She adjusts the underwear that's been moved out of place and rolls to her side. Her fingers float up the side of my face and whisk the long bangs of my wig out of my eyes, carefully removing the bobby pins before sliding the entire piece off my head. "You don't have to change a thing for me, Angie."

I place the camera on the bed. "I know."

She unbuttons the tight latex of my vest and my breasts spill out in relief. "We can develop it tomorrow."

My chest heaves in anticipation. "I'd like that."

A knowing smile curls on her face as she unzips my bottoms and peels them off. "I'd like to see what it is about me that inspired you to embrace a different destiny."

The cool air hits my thighs. "As if you don't already know."

I reach up for her, grasping the back of her neck, biting at her shoulder, wanting to pull her in. My body in another frenzy, needing to feel her skin against my skin. If only we could completely absorb one another...

She shifts back. "You're trying to make me fall in love with you, aren't you?"

"What? No, I mean, I—"

Her throat clears as she rolls away from me. "You don't want my type of love."

"That's not true. Why would you say that?" I reach for her but she stops me. "Love is for strangers and fools, and you and I are neither." She sits up. "I need to cool off. It's been another long, hot day at the office."

The muscles of her back flex as she fluffs out her hair.

I watch her leisurely stroll to the bathroom before laying my head back down, not willing to accept that she doesn't want what I thought she did all along.

SIXTEEN

She carefully manages the development process, explaining every step as she goes along like a veteran teacher. "If you don't have a darkroom, you can also do this in a black velvet bag," she says, unrolling the plastic film out of its case and feeding it back over something that looks like a hamster wheel. The dim red light we're in is a close enough equivalent to pitch darkness. I remember my dad telling me that.

"But you have to be careful. Any exposure to light will turn the film black."

I nod.

She even looks like a teacher in her loose jeans and stained white t-shirt, hair back in a messy ponytail. At least that's what I remember my industrial arts teacher looking like.

She hands me a container and then points to a jug. "That's the stock solution that processes the film. We're going to fill this tank with it."

Once the spindle with the roll of film drops into its counterpart, she seals it shut, the veins in her hands popping. I pour the solution through a hole at the top before screwing the last bit into place to completely close the container.

"It takes ASA 400 film ten minutes to develop."

After rotating and shaking the tank, she sets the timer and we wait.

I think about telling her that my parents have a darkroom and about my experience helping them develop photos from the most remote areas of the world, but she's in her element and I'm enjoying her this focused and subdued. Every detail is addressed with the precision of an artist.

"Your photography is very provocative," I tell her. My eyes scan the shelves for the photos of Rachel I found, but like the receipts in her drawer, they seem to have disappeared. "What drew you to the erotic arts?"

She rotates the tank again. "A fascination for what others consider taboo." She turns on the water and starts filling the sink. "Jean Agélou was one of the first to photograph women in the nude, even some sexual situations. They were considered so salacious at the time, that they could only be sold as postcards on the black market."

Cranking the faucet tightly to shut off the water, she tells me that Agélou mostly photographed prostitutes, who understood the value of being completely uninhibited.

I look down at my nipples perking through the similarly beat-up t-shirt she gave me to wear and tell her that not everybody is comfortable with being uninhibited.

Her eyes gaze in the same direction before she tests the temperature of the water. "If everybody understood the value of being uninhibited, the world would be a lot less obscene."

The timer sounds, and she tells me to rinse the film to stop the developer and then go through the same process using a fixer compound.

Dipping the film into the cool water, I wonder about the counter to that statement. If everybody was completely uninhibited, there might also not be any anticipation or build-up for what may come, and that chase is always half the fun. It's what draws people to test some unknown potential. That chase is what got me here, even if it was completely inadvert.

Once the film has been rinsed a second time, we clip it with a clothespin to the line strewn across the darkroom.

"We have to give it at least an hour to dry before we can make any prints," she says, setting the timer again.

We stare at each other through the dim red hue, at an impasse that in any other circumstance would be remedied by a suggestion of going to the mall or grabbing a bite to eat or a cup of coffee.

Her hand wipes a speck of water from my arm. "How about a movie?"

The light caress of her fingers on my arm sends my thoughts to an uninhibited place. "What do you like to watch?"

Her fingers continue their journey up my arm, across the rigid cotton, until they've reached my shoulder. She leans in, her warm breath against my ear. I reach for the edge of the counter to steady myself.

"Comedies," she finally spits out, laughing. "*Everything* can't be erotic in nature." She pulls me out of the darkroom. "The edges wouldn't be as intense."

A sense of humor is not something I would have expected from the master seductress. I have to believe she's being genuine right now. That she's liking me more than she wants to admit. That this isn't part of some malicious move.

The hefty remote control for the loft is at her fingertips again and just like every other time, with a few clicks and rearrangements, her space is transformed into a comfortable private movie theater.

Within twenty minutes, we're slouched on her couch, eating popcorn and watching old Laurel and Hardy silent movies. It's the first laugh I've had since this whole thing began and sharing it with Heather feels especially wholesome. Like we're best girlfriends hanging out on a typical weekend. Throwing popcorn at one another, imitating Hardy when he bonks Laurel on the head for doing something silly, and feeling like there's nowhere else we would rather be. And no one else we'd rather be with.

Catching a glimpse of what a normal relationship with Heather would be like makes me giddy. This is Heather, relaxed. Not worried about anyone barging in or trying to break out. Cracking extra salt over the popcorn, melting extra butter, because that's how I tell her I like it.

Every now and then I catch her observing, silently analyzing the way I sip the beer she offers. Still as suspicious of me as I am of her. But I try to assuage any doubt with slight affections, like stopping her fingers from nervously picking at the denim hole forming around her kneecap.

The timer in the darkroom buzzes. A rude intrusion to the moment we're sharing, but I'm also curious about the pictures I took on the roll of film.

The last few kernels of corn crunch between my teeth as I interrupt her reach for another handful. "Come on, I want you to see something."

Her bare feet plop on the concrete as *I* pull *her* this time, back into the darkroom and close the door.

Immediately recognizing the close-up of me and Heather lying on her bed towards the end of the roll, I unclip it from the string and ask for some scissors.

I take the pair she offers me, and this time, the fact that they're plastic only makes me smile. I snip the last negative, all the while listening to her instructions about how to read an image on the magnifier, which she decides to do for me.

After the image has been centered on the photo paper, Heather approximates the exposure time. I tell her to give it two extra seconds, to trust *me* this time, and she moves her hand away from the switch, no questions asked. I click it on and off, using my gut instinct.

Judiciously, the photo paper moves from bin to bin. Stopper, fixer, water rinse, until it's ready to be hung to dry. As the image begins to pop, I can already tell it's going to be a great shot.

"It's beautiful." I stare at the way the light in the photo hits her cheek, the shadows over the bed, my lips against her shoulder, eyes pinned on her with complete devotion. "I see a woman who's at peace and knows what she wants," I say. "A woman with possibilities far beyond the confines of her current life."

Her eyes drop away from the picture and she doesn't respond. Instead, she starts busying about with creating a contact sheet for the remaining thirty-five exposures. The statement has made her uncomfortable. "You see a vision of me. An ideal of something *you* want, or want to become."

"I see what we could be together," I say adamantly.

She shakes her head and hangs the contact sheet to dry next to the picture of us.

I play with a clothespin lying on the counter. Opening and closing it slowly, the creak of the small spring gnawing at me just like her resistance. "I know you've been through a lot and done a lot of messed up stuff, but it doesn't have to be that way."

Her gaze doesn't leave the contact sheet. "What else do you want to develop?"

I scan over the small versions of the photos I took delineating the topography of her body. "We can leave this place. Start somewhere new…together." My voice trails off.

There are four images at the very top of the contact sheet that aren't part of the series I took. It's Rachel. In this loft. She's smoking a cigarette at an opened window. A casual oversized men's shirt thrown over her otherwise naked body.

I shove one of the bins to the side, splashing solution onto my t-shirt. "Is she your girlfriend?"

"*Ex*-girlfriend," Heather clarifies.

My face flushes, from disbelief that she would be so careless, but also from a strange jealousy that maybe I was wrong about her reasons for locking Rachel in the Iron Maiden. If that was even the case. "That you still see on occasion?" I ask, even though we both know the answer.

"Yes." She doesn't lie.

I unclip the wet sheet. My grip slides through the sticky surface. "That you're still in love with. And that's why you won't leave with me."

She uncurls my fingers from the paper. "No. There are too many things I can't explain right now."

The contact sheet drops into a bin and the images begin to blur. "Like she gets you off better than I did last night?"

She reaches for the tongs because she's about to rescue the ruined contact sheet, but my hands clasp around her face forcefully, not giving her the chance. "Come on, Heather." I pull her into me. "Tell me what you need."

My face presses against hers, rubbing against the round of her cheekbone, the break of her nose, the tip of her chin, until my lips find her mouth. She braces against the counter as our tongues tangle in a dance of desire, moaning when I tug on her hair, hard. Inching down the uneven course of her jugular, my hands flow over her t-shirt, stroking the hard, bare nipples underneath. Our eyes lock as I gradually sink to my knees inhaling the leather scent of her belt, which I slowly unbuckle as she licks the bottom edge of her mouth and exhales sharply.

Without the belt, her jeans fall to the floor. I stop at the perfect circumference of her belly button to lick it once, twice, three times. The plastic bins scratch against the aluminum surface and the solutions slosh as she moves them aside so she can shift up onto the counter. I strengthen my grip around her waist as she lifts first one, then her other long leg to prop against the opposite wall of the narrow room. *This is what I really wanted to do to her yesterday.*

I bury my nose in the coarse hair of her pubic region, and the moment I run my tongue along the edge of her labia, her knuckles grasp the edge of the counter harder. I part her folds slowly so I can revel in her every pant and undulation. The briny tastes of her soft flesh and juices make my mouth water and thirst for more.

I begin a rhythmic stroke on one side of her clitoris and then the other, taking mental notes of her different replies. Eventually her pelvis thrusts into my face, rubbing up and down, until her legs begin to quake and she lets out a loud cry as a rippling spasm releases from her limbs.

First, her legs drop to the floor, and then her torso, to meet mine. A goofy grin lights her face. Similar to the one she had when we were watching all those black-and-white comedies. I reach to wipe some perspiration from her hairline, but she stops my hand and kisses it instead. "I need you, Angie. I need you."

We lock in an embrace on that floor, for a long while.

SEVENTEEN

A loud clap of thunder startles me out of my sleep. It echoes through the room. I look over to where Heather is lying. She's curled into a ball clasping a sheet tightly around her head. The rain beats heavily against the panes of glass.

She's trembling, and when I go to touch her arm, she retracts as if I've touched her with a pot of boiling water.

A long, spiny column of lightning illuminates the entire room. A large circle of blood stains the bed.

"Heather!" I gasp, shaking her.

Her head spins in all directions. "Angie?"

"Yes, it's me." I reach for her arm again, convinced something is horribly wrong. Her skin is moist and her t-shirt is drenched. "You...you're bleeding."

The tips of her fingers run across my every knuckle and crease. "It's my period." Her voice is breathy and her teeth clatter as she continues to clutch the sheet. "And my head...I need to call..."

"Call who?" I move my hand to her forehead, feeling for a

fever. *Does she want to call Rachel, or some other significant relationship she hasn't confessed yet?* "I'm here."

The rumble of thunder interrupts.

"In the medicine cabinet, there's some Butalbital for the migraine...and cramps." She curls tighter into a ball. "It's a handwritten label. Red container. The pads are under the sink."

I've heard how awful migraines can be. I scramble out of bed, pulling the t-shirt I was wearing yesterday over my head.

The wind howls through the rickety pane of the small bathroom window as I scan the medicine cabinet for the Buta-something. The handwriting on most of the containers is barely legible. My hand reaches for a red container as instructed. This is probably it, but I spot another red container on the shelf below it with writing that's too faded to read. I grab it as well. She can tell me which one is right.

I squat down and open the cabinet below the sink. There's a variety of feminine hygiene products to choose from. I grab a pad and a tampon, unsure of her preference. Regardless, she needs fresh underwear. Hands full, I head to the closet.

Remembering the bin filled with lingerie, I make my way over to it and start rummaging. Even the most sophisticated woman has underwear comfortable enough for that time of the month. Underwear that you don't mind ruining and hope your boyfriend never has to see.

Light, scratching noises from behind the wall make me stop my search. I drop the thong I'm holding and slowly slide over to *that* wall. *Is Rachel still in there?* I press my ear against the cool smooth partition as the storm wildly flexes its muscles. I don't hear anything discerning, just the sound of my heart beating loudly. *Do I call out her name?* Not with Heather in the other room. For all I know, the scratching is the family of rats I'm convinced live in the pleats of this building, or those cockroaches...

She wouldn't lock someone away like that. Not someone she has a relationship with. Not someone she loves.

My nails begin a rhythm of their own, up and down, to the left, to the right, like Morse code. The chalky paint is so old it's starting to chip in places.

Crack!

The bar of clothes above me falls.

I'm too petrified to scream. The garments suffocate. They're as heavy as dead weight. I shove them away, the jolt of adrenaline making my lungs fire rapidly, until I'm out from underneath the mess. I scamper back to the lingerie bin. My eyes close and my head leans against the plastic tub, trying to calm.

She's calling my name and it focuses me on why I'm in the closet. I yell back that everything is fine as I rummage more intently. *There must be something in here.* I finally find that something at the very bottom. Stretchy boy shorts that will get the job done for now.

"The clothes that were hanging in your closet fell," I explain, holding out the two red pill bottles, a maxi pad, a tampon, and the boy shorts.

She struggles to sit up, eyes darting and limbs unsteady. "Everything is bound to break eventually," she says.

I place the treasure trove next to her, helping her straighten. "There were two red containers in the medicine cabinet." One hand still steadying her, I reach for the pills. "I couldn't quite read what they said."

Her eyes blink rapidly and then she rubs them. Eventually, she reaches for the medicine, but her reach goes past the fistful of bottles I'm holding.

I bring my hand to her eye-level. "I'm not used to reading messy handwriting."

"B-U-T-A-B-I-T-A-L," she spells out, erratically, continuing to look past me.

"Why can't you just…" I guide her hand towards mine.

She breaks free, visibly upset.

"Because I can't—" Her forehead scrunches as she rubs her temples and rocks back and forth. "I can't see."

The statement sinks to the pit of my stomach. It devastates, like the first awareness that your parents are vulnerable. Bed-ridden with the flu, sobbing quietly in the bathroom, taking a verbal lashing from their spouse. You realize they're not superheroes, and that they won't always be able to take care of you. You get scared, but then an instinct kicks in and you try to help in whatever way you can, in the process becoming more independent.

I grip the plastic containers tightly, trying to decipher the handwriting so that I can somehow help her. One has a large letter B, but the rest of it…and the other one, it could be a D, then an R, yes, D-R-A. That's not it. It must be the first one. I press down on the top and twist it counter-clockwise vehemently, until it unscrews, shaking out a few pills into my palm.

"Open your hand," I urge her, until she finally trusts that the white oval medicines I place where her life line intersects her love line will make her better, not worse. She wolfs down two immediately before I have a chance to bring her water, but when I do, she gladly gulps it down.

I place the terrycloth I wetted in the kitchen against the inside of her thigh. At first she jumps, but then I start to gently wipe the dried red from her skin, and eventually she navigates my hand further up…into the creases of her vagina where life begins and ends in a hot, moist, welcoming femininity that's both violent and exquisite.

Another loud crack of thunder ricochets against the tall walls of the barren room, and I place the cloth in her hand so she can finish.

Peeling off the parchment-like slip from the back of the maxi pad and adhering it to the boy shorts, I'm amazed at this other level of intimacy developing between us.

"They're called ocular migraines," she clarifies, tossing the stained cloth to the floor as I help her step into the clean undergarment.

"You should take this off too," I say grasping her damp shirt. "I'll give you mine. It's dry."

She lifts her arms in agreement and I pull her t-shirt over her head.

"They're rare. Only one in two hundred migraine sufferers are affected," she continues to explain, but all I can do is fixate on the key hanging between her breasts.

The rain pounds against the windows as hard as my heart pounds in my chest. An uncomplicated escape plan is staring me right in the face.

"They're temporary," she stresses. "The blindness lasts anywhere from four to eight hours."

I barely register what she's saying, realizing that I don't have to convince her to love me or leave with me, or worry about how deep her loyalties to Rachel lie.

"But then it's over, and I'm back to full strength."

The flash of lightning illuminates the key like a dare. It's my chance. She's in pain, she can't see, she wouldn't have the same reflexes. She would fumble, fall, trip over her greatest attempts to stop me, but…she's shivering. I was supposed to give her my t-shirt.

Give her your t-shirt, Angie.

My fingers clasp onto the edge of the cotton. If I take this off, I'll have to bolt out of here naked. My mind is telling me not to put myself at her mercy again, but my heart is telling me something else.

I reach for the blanket at the foot of the bed and pull it over her shoulders instead.

"I envy you, Angie," she says, a pained look on her face. "You're about to burst from your cocoon. A young, beautiful butterfly with all the offerings of the world at your fingertips."

I tug the blanket across her chest, covering the key.

She descends to one side, her head hitting a pillow. "Some of us do more with that than others, but we never get a second chance." She curls into a ball again, this time more comfortable, and closes her eyes.

I look from the fallen star to the barrier blocking my freedom. She needs me. In more ways than one. *Can I be so cruel as to abandon her now?*

A draft at my back beckons me to reconsider and I turn towards the wall of windows. One is cracked open, and as I walk towards it, I can see the puddle of water that's formed on the concrete floor. I crank the handle so it closes.

I can't burst from my cocoon without her.

EIGHTEEN

My eyes snap open and focus on the moon now high in the clear sky. The rain has stopped and the loft is quiet except for the constant sweeping blades of the fan. Heather is lying still. Her breathing is even, her body is calm. I clasp onto her, shaken from the awful dream I just had.

I was walking a tightrope from one high-rise to another, to Heather who was on the other side. She was waving me toward her, telling me to keep my chin up and not look down and that everything would be all right. I did as she said. I cautiously placed one foot in front of the other, my concentration fixed on her, and when I got about three-quarters of the way across, I started feeling like I was going to make it all the way. I started feeling like *she* was going to help me get all the way across—until I saw her reach for a lever. It was the lever holding the rope tightly in place.

Knowing what she was about to do, I screamed for her to stop, but she yanked it to one side and the rope gave. It loosened beneath my feet, and I started falling, while she just looked on. Except it wasn't Heather anymore. It was Janelle. The long scraggly hair, the jawline that looked like it would fit better on a young man, the gangly arms built for an Olympic sport. She was a bit older now, but that devilish smile was the same.

One of her hands reached out to mine, and I clutched onto the tips of her fingers as tightly as a boa constrictor wraps around its prey, but then everything started sliding from my grasp. Fingernails slipped from their beds, skin stretched until its elasticity gave and the purple- and rose-hued structural tissues beneath became exposed. I kept grasping, but soon everything, including her, was too far from my reach.

I bury my face into Heather's back, breathing in her spicy scent. The blanket is now loose around her body, and I slide it down her shoulder and place my lips against her skin. She stirs and reaches for me. I crush into her harder, wanting to feel like she'll never let me down again. The way Janelle did.

Her body rotates, and I immediately synchronize with its comforting rhythm. The hard muscles of her back flex against my cheeks, and her hand tugs on my leg to pull it further between hers. My hand grazes the skin just below her ribcage and she lets out a sigh. Her hand grabs my hair and I bite down on her neck. The heat between us momentarily melts all my doubts and fears about staying when I had a chance to leave.

She hauls me on top of her. Eyes clear, tongue running across lips, debilitation gone. She's in control again. My breasts feel full and sore like I'm about to start *my* period. *Touch me, lick me, pleasure me.* I'm starting to think it's all I care about anymore.

The moment she starts to handle them, I feel a gush of euphoria. And when she tears off my t-shirt and buries into them, plucking my nipples, my pussy clenches.

Now her hands are on my butt cheeks, squeezing them, pulling me into her as she thrusts her pelvis. My clit hardens and I grind against her pubic bone as her fingers glide down the crack of my behind, finding that sensitive place.

"You're so wet," she says, lightly moving her fingers up and down my labia.

"You always make me wet." I can barely get the words out. My head is spinning with thoughts of her taking me over another brink, completely freeing me from my cocoon. My hips rock back, urging for more.

Her fingers move up and find a different sensitive spot. This time I don't tense up.

She retracts and cautiously caresses the tops of my thighs.

"I know you didn't want to stay here...with me." There is distress in her eyes. "But I need to know that's changed. For the right reasons."

My body is so riled up, I don't want to think about all that right now...what could've been if we'd met under different circumstances, or hadn't experienced all those horrible things. I just want us to be lovers and forget everything else. "I didn't leave yesterday, because..." I flip my hair. The tips sweep her neck. "I need you as much as you need me."

She pins my hair behind my ear. "I love you, Angie. Whatever happens with us, I want you to know that."

The statement has a cautionary tone, but it also melts me inside. Erik hasn't said those words yet. No one has. I know they can be used so flippantly, but Heather has nothing to gain by lying right now.

This was my plan, and yet I don't feel like she's fallen into anything without giving it a lot of thought. My lips fall against hers, and the longer we kiss, the more I realize I feel the same way...

Wanting lips part from mine. "Do you trust me?"

I look down at the woman who has fractured me emotionally and physically so many times in such a short period. The woman I want to escape from one minute, and in the next am not sure I'm baiting anymore because the emotions feel too real. "Why do you need my permission now?"

I watch her reach for a remote, point it off in a distance, and press a button. "I want to give you something." The tiniest of red lights blinks off to black. "I want you to be open to it."

This is just between us now. "Heather, whatever it is that we're doing here right now, I trust it. I trust you."

When she gets off the bed, her face brightens, like she has a new lease on life. The remote is placed back on the end table and she almost skips to the other end of the loft.

I spread out seductively, grinning, ready for her to take me in as many ways as she knows how.

She takes her time to prepare, but I'm not nervous this time. When she emerges, I can tell that she's wearing that harness again and a dildo. But it looks different this time. It's smaller and smoother, without the ridges designed to resemble a large vascular membrane. Her hands are clutching some other toys too. I refrain from asking what they are because I want to be surprised.

"You need to turn over now." The softness is gone from her eyes.

I do as I'm told.

She slides a bulky pillow under my hips and then walks around the bed, tugging my wrists together and binding them with something velvety soft. The fabric is then pulled through one of the rings around a bedpost for extra measure.

My face is down in the sheets and my behind is high in the air. I'm suddenly aware that it's the centerpiece of her bed, but I dare not fidget.

The hum of a vibrator breaks the silence.

She wraps my hands around her cock. "Do you like that?"

I've never used a vibrator before or seen one quite like this. It tickles my palms, but I like the way it feels. I nod.

"Do you want to feel that inside of you?"

I tighten my grip. "I do."

She jerks her vibrating cock out of my hands and climbs back on the bed. I feel it at the entrance of my slit. The rapid pulsation is almost too much at first, but she takes her time with it, gradually moving it along the length of my opening and then sliding it forward until it reaches my clit. Nerve endings ignite like Christmas lights.

I move up and down the length of it, the constant vibration making me sore, but also making me grind down harder until the soreness gives way to numbness and an orgasm starts to build.

The climax is a quick and electrifying burst, like fireworks, and as soon as it ends, I shift away, the sensitivity almost unbearable. But she grabs onto my hips.

"This is just the beginning, baby," she says, as she lands a smack on my rear. The brand stings, reminding me of my place, but I don't mind. "Do you hear me?" She smacks my backside again.

"Yes," I say, nodding rapidly. Already in a trance that I never want to leave. *You can be free here. Free to do whatever you want and be whoever you want.* Those words she said when I first stepped through her door resonate in my mind clearly now.

She directs her vibrating cock between my wet folds and deftly pushes it inside. It feels robust and intense as it reawakens every inch of me.

Her hands pinch my skin and my face rubs against the cotton of her sheets as the pulsation increases in frequency.

I clamp down around it and groan as my body seizes the full effect of this machine.

"I want you to come for me again, baby," she says as she moves one of her fingers to my other opening. It's back there again, but this time everything is slicker and her finger pops in with ease.

That tiny nudge is all I need to give way to another explosion that makes me bellow as my body quakes under her.

The vibration stops and she pulls out of my throbbing slit. I collapse onto the pillow under me. I'm completely exhausted, physically and emotionally.

"I know what you want, Angie," her voice coos, "and that's what I want to give to you."

My heart races. I know what she means. *Am I really ready to do this now?* I catch a glimpse of her reflection in the windowpanes. That mane of hair, strong body, harness over her hips...

Yes.

I refuse to stop like I did with Erik because of lines in the sand I keep drawing for myself. *I'm not just some conservative prude obsessed only with getting assignments in on time and maintaining a 3.5-plus grade-point average.*

Something cool and wet coats my rectum and her finger slips in a little deeper this time.

She continues to smoothly ply first one, then two fingers inside and I feel a vibrator at my clitoris again. This one is smaller, different from the apparatus hanging from her waist. It nips gently at my clit as her fingers continue to stretch me.

The sensation is almost unbearable, but at the same time, I don't want it to stop. I buck towards her. So close…so deliciously close. *Push it in deeper, make it hurt more, take me to places I never knew existed*…but she slowly pulls out of me.

I pant and stare at the binds around my arms, on an excruciating edge, realizing how completely beholden I am to her.

I feel the outline of the rubber dildo against my behind. "It's that bit of fear that makes the outcome so good," she says, running her fingers like raindrops up my back. "That bigness and fullness… it's that unknown that takes you to new heights. I promise." She grips the back of my neck. "I promise."

My entire body is pulsing with anticipation as I feel more wet stuff and the head of her dildo at my rear.

It starts pushing in me. It's bigger than her fingers, but I want it to be. I'm opening and she's driving, splitting me like an atom, and I know an unbelievable amount of energy is about to release.

My eyes tear up and I bite down on the sheet under me. I feel the shaft push in deeper and deeper, until I hear her tell me it's all the way in, baby. I release the sheet between my teeth and inhale deeply. The apparatus inside of me starts a low, temperate pulsation that elates my entire lower regions as another buzzing sensation vibrates at my clitoris.

With each achingly slow thrust in and out, my mind breaks through another set of barriers I never thought it would. Eventually any hurt is replaced by a volatile hunger that my body flexes around.

As her rhythm starts increasing, my body starts releasing like it never has before. I cry out wildly, instinctually, unleashing a climax that reverberates through every inch of my core.

When it stops, she oh-so-gently pulls out of me again. "You were amazing to watch, baby. So beautiful...so free."

She drops to her side and unties the soft fabric around my wrists. The pillow is pulled out from under me. We hold each other close.

"I love you too, Heather."

My body is trembling.

NINETEEN

The next morning, I wake to the scents and sounds of Heather cooking in the kitchen. I feel like I've been asleep for days and like it's the best sleep I've had in weeks.

I stretch luxuriously and notice a light silky robe draped over the footboard of the bed. I reach for it and can tell it's well-worn. The fabric has a few stains and the material is thinning out in spots. I throw it over me and slide off the bed.

Finding Heather in a domestic role is surreal. She's wearing a slip that is the same cream color and vintage as my robe, as she whisks eggs and tends to some strips of bacon in the frying pan.

"Good morning," I say to alert her, but when I look up at the clock, it's well after one in the afternoon.

"You look like you slept well," she says, mixing ingredients in a glass measuring cup.

I tell her I did and then offer to help, but she tells me to sit down and pours me a cup of coffee.

I take a sip without hesitation and continue to watch her work.

The finished product is an impressive and elaborate effort. Fresh fruit sits next to sautéed asparagus with onions, mushrooms, eggs, and bacon over brioche. Everything drips in hollandaise sauce. I wonder where it all came from. Last time I looked in her fridge, it was bare except for some butter, bread, and a carton of orange juice.

She places a plate of food in front of me, and my appetite roars back for the first time since I got here. The utensils and serving ware are still all paper and plastic. *We'll go shopping and pick out proper kitchen stuff one of these days.*

I create what looks to be a perfect morsel of flavors and bite down. My mouth is exhilarated. "Do you do this often?"

She looks at me like I've asked a loaded question. "Actually, I've never done this before."

I tilt my head. "Cooked in general, or cooked for someone?"

"Neither, really." I watch her carefully slice a piece of asparagus with her plastic knife. "I've never cared enough to."

I continue shoveling food in my mouth. "Not for any girlfriend…or boyfriend?" I'm genuinely curious. I can't imagine that her only romantic interests have been the Lolita relationship with her uncle, and the girlfriend she now locks away in an Iron Maiden.

She shakes her head and finishes chewing her vegetables. "Look, Angie, there've been a lot of girls and even a couple of guys I've had sexual relationships with." She drops several scoops of sugar into her coffee.

I fold each finger around my own coffee mug with precision. "And Rachel."

She stops stirring. "I've known Rachel for a long time, but our relationship has changed."

"Changed because you don't sleep together anymore?" I sound like a jealous love interest.

"We eventually have to give in to our needs."

The way Heather looks at me…it makes me think of last night and how wild it was.

"It was time for something different." She starts stirring again, swiftly this time. The cockiness is gone from her expression. "But I don't know if it even makes sense." She pulls the spoon out and slams it down on the thick wood. "I shouldn't have bothered—"

I put my hand over hers. "No, Heather. It's wonderful what's happening between us. And it means a lot to me that you would do all this." I make a sweeping gesture at the breakfast. I know it hasn't been easy for her to open up to me. I appreciate that too.

I pick up my utensils and we continue eating in silence.

I clear my throat and take a sip of coffee. "I'm going to break up with him."

She looks at me, confused.

"Erik. I'm going to break up with him," I tell her, clarifying my intentions. "I want us to have a real chance." My fingers fold around hers. "If you let me." Part of me can't believe the words are coming out of my mouth—but it's the truth. I can't imagine going back to a relationship with Erik after everything I've experienced with Heather. I don't even care when I get to leave her loft. I've already missed handing in an assignment and a couple of quizzes, and for the first time in my life I don't care. What's a few more days, or even a week? For the first time in my life, I'm getting to explore a part of myself I never thought I would. And I know I can't do it without her.

A brightness creeps over her face and she walks around the butcher block table to where I'm sitting. She cups my face in her hands and starts kissing me. Her mouth presses hard against mine, her tongue ferociously invading and her fingers pinching my cheeks, as if to make sure I'm real.

My arms embrace the body I've been attracted to since I first laid eyes on it, feeling her solid outlines through that slinky top and her firm skin. I start dragging her back to the bed between our beseeching kisses. My hunger for food has been replaced with my hunger for her.

She unties the sash holding my robe together as we fall back on the bed and explore each other's bodies under a newly negotiated contract.

Her palms cup my breasts and she licks each nipple. I moan with urgency, running my hands along her sculpted behind, driving it between my legs and lifting the slip over her head. We press into each other, the desire between us becoming more fervent.

We spend the rest of the day making love. Unable to stop, like an addiction you don't want to curb. Every now and then, we nibble on some leftover breakfast or rest in the comfort of each other's arms, until the sun has dipped far enough to warrant turning on a lamp.

The hue of the incandescent bulb warms the room and she rolls onto her back with a joint and a lighter in her right hand. With a click and an exhale, smoke begins to weave through the soft glow. We lie on top of the covers for a while, just gazing up at the way the fan perfectly serenades our thoughts with each rotation.

This time when she passes the joint to me, I don't decline. The first drag hits my throat and lungs sharply and I cough, but almost immediately, I feel a calm euphoria swim through my head.

"Have you ever been with a woman before?" Her voice trails into the figurines of dragons and flowers forming in all the smoke.

I tell her I have. That I was young. "We would kiss sometimes.

And sometimes I wished we'd done more." A shy smile creeps over my face and I turn away from her slightly. "When she moved with her parents, I felt like part of me was missing. For a long time."

Heather folds a pillow in half and rests it under her head. "She was your first love."

"I didn't know it at the time. And later, I don't think I wanted to admit that was the case. But yes, she was."

More smoke cascades through the air, but it only makes my vision clearer. Nothing ever fit right because I was on the wrong path with the wrong person—not because I was overweight.

"What about a threesome?" she interrupts my thoughts. She tells me that Erik seems like the kind of guy who'd make that his first request.

I laugh and shake my head. "Erik is *so* not like that. He's a jock. More interested in game strategies and working out."

Not that I didn't think he'd had opportunities and maybe even tried. He was certainly good-looking enough to attract that kind of attention. But as self-conscious as I was about my looks, he was just as self-conscious in the bedroom—at least with me. He'd grab and suck with such haste, like he was expecting arousal to happen in two seconds, and if it didn't, he'd get frustrated instead of asking questions. And I didn't really know how to direct him around my body. I barely knew how to direct myself. Except for his graduation night...

"Does he watch porn?"

"Don't we all?"

I'm feeling brash now, and I tell her about the night of his graduation. How I started taking those pictures of us being intimate, and how after the ceremony and parties, Erik passed out drunk on the bed, but I wasn't tired so I looked at the pictures we'd taken.

Most of them were indecipherable. Blurred or too close, like a smattering of clothes on skin. I found a few, though, that really captured how in sync our bodies were that night. It turned me on, how close I'd come, how engaged he was. My hand started to wander between the slit of my dress. But I needed more. More than just him, and me, and us.

"I found this website," I tell her, passing the smoldering stub back to her. "Stone Media, LLC. Like nothing else I'd seen before."

Her head perks up. She wants to know more about this exceptional adult portal.

"For members only." I lay my head back down on the pillow and fold my legs. "That's what the screen said and then listed all these crazy pricing options." I tell her the monthly memberships started at ten grand and worked up to the six-figure range. "If you filled out your first and last name, you could check out teasers. So I did. Well, not using my name, but Erik's."

The exhale of smoke stops escaping her mouth. "Why would you do that?"

"I don't know." I start rubbing some black debris from the silk of my robe, so much it heats my fingertips. "The idea was making me excited, and I wanted to see more—"

"Did you want *him* to see more?" she cuts me off.

"I don't know. It was his computer, so I thought it made sense." This is my simple answer, though at the time I'm sure my reasoning was more complex. "Someone tried to get me to sign up after a while."

She raises an eyebrow and hands the joint back to me.

"This messenger window popped up and startled me," I continue to explain, my lips wrapping around the crushed moist paper. "It wasn't automated. Someone on the other side wanted to strike a deal with me. Wanted to show me more of something I kept looking at." I inhale deeply, and the exiting smoke feels like the last of my reservations leaving with it.

She turns on her side and jabs through the smooth swirls with her hands. "What did you keep looking at?"

"A blonde and a brunette entangled in one another on a bed. The blonde obviously had more experience and was guiding the brunette through ever-increasing stakes of ecstasy, like a sexual coming-of-age novel. As the kinks became more intense, the dominant one had to be more purposeful with earning the submissive's trust." I pass the smoldering stub back to her. "They ended up doing what we did last night."

My eyes don't shy away from hers. I want her to know how much last night meant to me. "It was the intensity between them…not just what they were doing. That's what really took me over the brink."

That's also when I closed the lid. And maybe that's why Erik began acting more distant. Saw the site I'd visited. Saw something he didn't like, or couldn't explain. Or maybe it turned on something in him, like it did in me, that he needed to think about.

Black has deposited on the tips of her fingers too. She brings them closer to her lips. "Intensity isn't something you can just create between two people." She sucks deeply.

"I know. That's why this site…the women weren't just pretending. Getting jack-hammered and making the noises you do to make a man feel like he's accomplishing something. The lovemaking was elaborate, gritty, even violent. But it all eventually led to a real climax."

The ash end of the joint falls on the pillow under her, and I brush away the powdery debris. *"Eventually,"* I continue. "Some of the stuff looked like the climax was a literal ending. That's why when that messenger window popped up again, I thought it might be the cops. Some kind of trap."

She lets out a laugh and then leans over to rub her lower back. One of her nipples pops out of the old slip she's wearing. Her eyes regard the display with amusement. Lashes lowered, they drift to my chest.

"You would fill it out better than me," she says, grazing a finger along my breast. "But I can't seem to let it go." She takes another deep inhale of the joint. "It's the only thing I took from my mother…well, after she kicked me out," she snickers, exhaling slowly. "I'd always admired the way she looked in it."

"Why did she kick you out?"

"She walked in on us. Me and Johnny. Guess we'd gotten a little sloppy, or too caught up, and didn't notice the time." She passes the joint back to me. "But she didn't lash out at *him*. Oh no! *I* was the temptress, the serpent, the whore." She plays with the lace near her strap. "And he just stood there, taking my mother's side, agreeing that I had seduced him. Didn't do a damn thing to help me. Not even when I dropped out of eleventh grade and was living under a bridge and starving. I found his address in the phone book, and he wouldn't even let me stay for a night. Just told me to do what I knew how to do best and it'd get me by."

Her eyes look hollow. Haunted by a distant memory that clings like a red wine stain on a white shirt no matter how many times it's washed.

I ask her if she's okay, but she doesn't answer. Just stares at me. Stares at the way I now hold the joint, and how I cock my head to get the hair out of my eye, and how I turn from my side to my stomach and kick my legs up.

She takes the joint from my fingers and puts it between my lips. "I think you'll prefer being with a woman in the long run."

I inhale, my expanding lungs filling with a warm nectar that pervades my brain with lofty ideals, then exhale, smirking.

I think she's right.

She picks at a crust of food that's dried onto her slip and tells me there's a trust between women that can never be there with a man. We think alike, we go through similar experiences. It's easier for a man to take advantage of you and use you, because they're controlled by different instincts. "They'll sell you out if they have to...the way Uncle Johnny did."

The robe slips down from my shoulders and she reaches to adjust it, brushing my skin. She takes the joint out of my mouth.

I don't know if I completely agree with her. "I'm sorry you never met a man worthy of your love. I know they exist."

I truly believe that. My dad is one of them. I remember my mother once leaving us for a year when I had just entered high school, in the name of an archeological dig. Many arguments led up to her departure. It was an opportunity of a lifetime, she said, but someone needed to stay home with me.

My father fought her for a long time—he particularly didn't like that she was going with another man—but he eventually stopped. A year later she came home, and they went on living the way they always had, no questions asked. It was as if the bump in the road had never happened, or that they'd expected it to happen. They dealt with it—like you'd deal with a flat tire.

Sometimes I thought Erik and I had what it took to last that long, even though I saw signs that made me wonder whether we were a good fit at all. But we'd had moments...like that ridiculous talent contest he made me do with him to help raise money for his water polo team. I thought it was going to be a disaster, but instead I impressed him with my singing ability and he impressed me with his guitar-playing skill. We did a rock satire of a few *Phantom of the Opera* songs and ended up winning. It made me believe in us.

The memory makes me laugh out loud and Heather asks what I'm thinking about. I start telling her an abbreviated version of the story, until the look on her face changes. It hurts her to know that I still think of him. She brought me here because she knew I was vulnerable and curious about being with a woman…no, not any woman—just her. Now she wants more from me. And I want to give her more.

"Look, it doesn't change things. I'm still going to break up with him." I put my hand on her arm and squeeze it reassuringly.

The joint almost falls from her mouth. "I know." She extinguishes it on the wooden end table.

I watch her, watching *me*…wanting me, and move my hand up to caress her cheek. She leans into me and I move my fingers to her lips, feeling the cracks and parting them so I can feel the wetness inside.

She sucks on my fingers and rubs her thighs together. The familiar flame between us still giving off heat below the tiring embers. I reach deeper into her mouth and she bites, teasing. I intertwine them in her mess of hair instead. We smile at one another and I tip toward her, placing my lips gently on hers.

I run my tongue along the perimeter of her mouth, moistening it. She's already trembling, breathing erratically, twisting her hips. She needs a release.

I push her back and roll on top of her. My breasts tumble out from the robe, sweeping against the silk and lace of her slip.

I continue kissing her as the perspiration mounts between our legs. Everything is slick, including her delicious snatch. I rotate my fingers around it, still getting used to pairing her responses with my touch, but maybe the high is making it easier this time. When I sense her movements becoming more urgent, I continue that circular motion around her sensitive nub.

She grips me, muscles straining, breath quickening, until the release comes with an audible quake. She grows limp under me. There's so much more I want to do to her...

I rest my head on her shoulder, the high now lulling me to sleep.

"Angie, are you awake?" Her voice beckons me back.

"I am," I reply, groggy.

She strokes my hair and my lids grow heavy. "Before you break up with Erik, and we...I need you to do one more thing for me tomorrow."

"What is it?" I can barely concentrate on what she's saying.

"I need your help with another video."

My mind wanders from the safe place that's just been created to one that feels darker again. I look up at her and can tell she's uneasy. I had meant to ask her more about the videos and the pictures and even Rachel, but somehow it started to feel less like a priority. Or maybe I just didn't want to know. "What kind of video?"

She plays with the cuff of my robe. "I...I just need you to trust me."

We've come too far to turn back now. "Alright. Whatever you need."

TWENTY

The loft is dark, except for the cluster of red, white, and blue lights aimed at her latest set, and me.

I'm sitting in a chair with my hands cuffed behind my back, in front of a long metal table. Like something you'd see in an interrogation room at a police station.

A microphone dangles from a long chord centered over the table and a large unframed mirror rests on a wall off to my right. When I look into it, I see myself made up like a streetwalker.

My hair is teased and sprayed, my eyes are dark like a raccoon's, and my lips are overdone in a bright fuchsia. My breasts are popping out of a push-up bra and torn white tank top, and a pink stretch skirt barely covers my behind.

The look was at her request, before she told me she had to put in a half-day at the office. And when she returned, she wasn't happy. It wasn't extreme enough, she said, and helped my look along by adding more black around my eyes, more pink to my lips, and ripping the tank top further down the middle. The briskness in her voice and actions made me wonder whether she was really that upset about my costuming attempt, or something else.

I'm trying not to take it all too seriously. She obviously has a fascination for role-play and kink, and it would make little sense to judge that now. I just don't understand why *that* has to be on. The familiar red recording light of the camera blinks at me in the distance.

I tried to get her to open up about the videos this morning over breakfast, which felt different from yesterday's. Her demeanor was more formal as she placed the usual butter and jam in front of me and hurriedly popped two pieces of bread in the toaster.

She refused to give out any pertinent details when I started quizzing her about who and what the videos were for. She tried only to assure me that the videos were like the pictures, for her own personal use. She just liked to document things, she repeated several times.

I continued to press her as I sipped on the coffee she'd slid across to me. I reminded her that part of loving someone was being honest with them. But it was no use. She said that one day she would tell me everything, before kissing me on the cheek, throwing two pieces of partially burnt toast on my paper plate, and walking out to put in her half-day at some office I still knew nothing about. A half-day that felt lonely and uninspired. *Why would my looking like a streetwalker turn her on that much?*

She exits her dressing room wearing large mirrored aviator sunglasses and a cop hat that's tilted to one side. A uniform-blue shirt is tied around her midriff and a short black skirt hugs her hips.

A stack of files are tucked neatly under her arm, and she fingers the familiar key hanging around her neck.

She stops opposite me, at the other end of the table, and fingers the holster around her waist. I notice it secures the stun gun. She whips off her shades and drops the files. "You're in a lot of trouble, aren't you?"

"I don't know—"

"Picked up for solicitation," she cuts me off. "And it's not the first time, is it?"

I chew on the stick of gum she gave me earlier as part of my outfit, not knowing what to say. We didn't rehearse anything. She just told me to act like a hooker and that she was going to play a cop and then got busy setting up the room. Tensely, like she wasn't enjoying it as much as the other times.

She walks around to where I'm seated and takes out the wooden baton slung at her other side. "I'm asking what you have to say for yourself?" she sneers, hitting my knuckles harder than expected.

"Ow!" I yell out, trying to soothe my fingers. "Don't hurt me, Officer. I'll do anything you want." I deliver this line in a high-pitched voice, like I imagine the bimbo version of me would.

She leans over, twisting and tugging at one of my nipples. "Are you trying to bribe a police officer?"

"If that's what you wanna call it. I'm just hoping we can both have a good time," I say with ridiculous zest, arching back so that my breasts completely spill out onto the table.

She slithers in close to my ear, her one hand kneading an exploited breast, her other one reaching down between my legs, gripping me hard. "Good Time's your middle name, isn't it, sweetheart?"

Her fingers start to circle over my underwear in that way that only she knows how, and her closeness and that scent…

I throw my head against her shoulder and gyrate my hips around her hand. "Are you waiting for a handshake to seal the deal?"

She shoves herself off me. "While I applaud your enthusiasm, there's some paperwork we need to settle up first."

She struts away and opens the file she dropped earlier. After rummaging for a few moments, she slides some photographs across the table.

The pictures are of me and Erik.

Those private, intimate moments at his desk on graduation day that no one should ever have been privy to. In some, we're kissing, in others, completely engrossed in the act. There are shots of him handling my breasts, hiking up my dress…of me unzipping his pants. I'm aghast. Speechless.

I watch as she thumbs through papers. "He belongs to the Delta Pi fraternity, well-known for its VIP memberships at strip clubs, soliciting phone-sex operators and…persons such as yourself for private parties. He's even visited an exclusive website called Stone Media, LLC. Several times." She flips the manila folder closed.

My nostrils widen as I deeply inhale. The old, exposed wood in the room becomes a stench rather than an aperitif. I am suddenly aware of the unyielding heat winning over the meager fan's attempt to cool and the odor of unwashed sweat from sheets and bodies. Pheromones jostled from the heights of ecstasy and at the same time the instinct to survive.

"You're familiar with that website, aren't you?" Her fingers glide along the tattered edges of the folder.

She starts spinning her baton as she walks back over to me. "And here *you* are, in all sorts of compromising positions with him." She bats the table. "Can you tell me the exact nature of your relationship?"

My mind races, trying to sort out facts that don't add up to anything. *Are we still acting, or not?* Nothing makes sense right now. "He...he's just a friend."

She lifts her baton and places it under my chin. "Are you sure that's *all* you are? Because his Facebook page boasts an entire photo album dedicated to his 'sweet new girlfriend' with pictures of someone who looks an awful lot like your alter ego. If I find out later there's something more going on, any plea bargains will be off the table." The wood presses hard into my throat. "Solicitation is a serious offense."

I jerk my head away from the stick. "So is entrapment. How did you get all those pictures?"

"I did a little bit of research. Found out all sorts of things about your...friend. Like the fact that not only did he visit Stone Media, LLC, several times, but he also bought a membership."

That doesn't sound like Erik at all. Even if I forgot to shut down the browser with that website, he wouldn't get involved. He might check it out like I did, but not buy a crazy expensive membership.

I go on the offensive. "*You* did a little research, or the hacker you bailed out of jail a month ago did? Or maybe you had your ex do some dirty bidding for you?"

She lowers the baton and walks closer. "What else do you think you've pieced together about me?"

I hesitate, confused and hurt. I thought we were past all this, but she's obviously still hiding something from me. "That you're a serpent disguised as a beautiful woman."

She forces my head to the table. "And you're completely innocent?" She moves the baton across my neck. "*You* weren't looking for trouble, were you?" The baton presses tighter. "*You* weren't trying to find someone, were you?" It's closing off the oxygen running down my throat. "It was all this *other* person, this serpent?"

My head throbs and I gasp for air. She releases the baton and yanks me up by the hair. I look at the red light of the camera, having a hard time believing that this is all part of some personal documentary.

"Heather, I don't want to play this game anymore. I told you I was going to break up with Erik so that we could be together. What else do you want me to do?"

She jerks my hair and flings off her sunglasses. Her eyes are completely cold. "Look at that," she says increasing her volume. "Underneath it all, you're just a common, cheap, pathetic whore... willing to say and do anything it takes to get out of a situation."

The statement stings.

"Aren't you?" she demands.

I close my eyes so I don't have to look at her.

"Aren't you?!"

I feel like she's going to rip my hair out. "Why are you doing this to us?!" I scream out. "I thought you loved me!"

She lets go of me and sets down the baton. "I love everything that brings me one step closer to solving a problem," she snickers, "with a boyfriend."

A knot of nerves forms in my stomach. I'm furious with myself for believing that anything she said last night was real.

She smacks me across the face. "I saw the way your eyes lit up when you saw pictures of him. I know you've been trying to contact him!"

She smacks me again, harder. "Tell me you're not just doing

whatever it takes so that I drop all charges against you and let you out of here. So that you can go live happily ever after with *him*."

I remain stoic.

She pulls out a switchblade from one of the front pockets of her skirt and sticks it at my neck. "What's the matter—not having a good time anymore?" The sheath slides across my flesh like nails on a chalkboard.

"You can't intimidate me anymore!" I explode, seething with anger. "You want to kill me? Go ahead. You want me to tell you everything was a lie? I won't."

My emotions crumble around me. Not even twenty-four hours ago, I actually considered staying here with her. I considered breaking up with Erik over a slew of complicated reasons and trying something different, *with her*. Now all I want to do is…grab that switchblade and twist it 'til it breaks her wrist. Slide the blade out and pull it across her vocal chords, puncturing her artery with one fell one swoop, and watch the blood drain silently from her neck.

She sets the switchblade on the table next to the baton and pulls the chain with the key over her head.

I stare at what she dangles in front of me. I look at the stun gun secured at her hip.

"You're free to go," she says matter-of-factly, placing the key on the table. Her fingers toy with the zipper on the side of her skirt. "Well, almost. There's one more thing—"

"You told me this video was the last thing."

"I invited my friend over later tonight," she continues, ignoring me. "You remember him, don't you?"

She lifts my face and runs her fingers along my lips. "He wants to meet you." She pinches my cheek. "It's not a lot to ask, is it?"

The videos and pictures are for the city inspector. That's the only explanation. Otherwise, why would he care to meet me? He didn't so much as sniff in my direction when he decimated her loft, and her. It was all about her…until she showed him something else he might like. A new exchange for paying the bills.

I look at the key. If my hands weren't cuffed, it would be within reach and I wouldn't have to agree to anything. I wouldn't hesitate this time either. I would snatch everything on the table and fight my way to the door, even if I died trying.

"No, of course not. Whatever you want me to do," I say indifferently. "Just a little meet and greet, maybe a little adult fun. Why not? May as well go out with a bang."

The thought disgusts me.

"Go out with a bang," she says, peering at me. "That's a good one." Cavalierly, she struts away.

My heart races. I can't let her leave, or get *him,* before I have a fighting chance. I have to get her attention. I need to get out of these cuffs.

"You know what's even better?" I shout at her.

Planting a heel, she slowly turns to face me.

"Getting me out of these cuffs, so…" I think quickly. "So I can show you the kind of whore I *really* am."

She taps her fingers on the table.

"We wouldn't want some *man* to come between us now, would we?" I smack my gum.

She reaches cautiously for the ring of keys attached to a belt loop, her eyes scrutinizing me as she walks around the back of my chair.

"Yeah, you know me." My chewing becomes more exaggerated. "Whatever I need to do to get out of here."

I feel her stick a key into the lock of my cuffs, but then stop. "Wait a minute…"

I pray that she doesn't change her mind.

"What happens if you disappoint me?"

"I haven't disappointed you yet, have I?" My voice is dripping with seduction.

I hear the lock click open and the cuffs loosen. I shake them off me and they hit the floor with a loud thud.

She steps around me and we're back to our stand-off. "Alright. Show me whatcha got."

Knowing what I have to do makes the adrenaline burst through my veins.

I leap for the key on the table.

She draws the stun gun, but I'm faster than her this time and grab her arm. I twist and slam it down on the table with everything I have. I snatch the switchblade and start stabbing at her limb.

She screams.

I keep stabbing anywhere I can. Blood spurts onto my face. It only makes me more determined. Suddenly, the knife stakes through her hand. I feel it go through her skin, muscle, tendons, everything, and penetrate the wood beneath. I watch with wonder as her perfection melts into a disfigured mess.

Her screams dissolve into sobs as her open hand reaches for the switchblade.

I grab the baton.

She drops to her knees, clinging to the table.

Every instinct tells me to strike her in the head, knock her out, maybe even for good. The key sweats in my hand. I look down at her, cowering, crying…

"No, Angie, please don't. Please don't leave." She holds out a shaking hand to me. "I'm sorry."

I drop the baton and turn for the front door.

I try to run, but stumble, so I kick off the ridiculous high heels. I continue on, picking up the pace, looking back only once, to make sure she's still pinned.

I reach the door, open my hand, and trembling, raise the key to the lock.

The key pushes in and I yank it clockwise.

It won't turn.

I take the key out. It drops. As I bend to pick it up, I hear her wail for me to not leave.

I try the key the other way. It still doesn't turn. My hands feel sloppy, my ears are ringing, and I'm having a hard time focusing. I force the key in every direction until I'm forced to accept that it's not going to work. It's not the right key.

Something hits me in the back and I drop forward. The key falls out of my hand.

I look up.

There she is. Her mangled arm dangles at her side, but her eyes are calm. She bashes my legs with precision, knowing exactly how to incapacitate me. When I'm completely down, she holds the baton high over her head with her good arm. This time it's her chance to finish me off for good.

She drops the baton and falls to the floor next to me, wrapping her arms around me. Red stains my skin and clothes.

I begin to cry uncontrollably, like a child who's just been crudely punished.

She holds me tight, caressing me and cooing, trying to soothe.

I continue to cry, unable to contain myself. "Y…you, li…lied," I stammer.

"No, baby, I didn't lie to you."

"The key…it was…"

She takes what's left of my tank top and wraps it around her oozing hand to stanch the bleeding. "I knew you would fight being with him. I knew you loved me too much. If I thought you didn't, I would have given you the real key. I promise I would have." She pulls me in again. "And now we're so close." She starts rocking me back and forth. "So close to being together. Forever."

I lay into her, too tired to fight.

TWENTY-ONE

I wake up missing Erik. The simplicity of our relationship. The way he grabs onto my hip in the morning like an anchor, pulling me in and rubbing his stubble against my back until I tell him to stop, and then he grabs onto me tighter, growling as he rubs with more fervor, like he's polishing something with fine sandpaper, until I yelp out that it hurts. It's the gesture I look forward to the most when we spend the night together.

Bruises have formed on my legs, and every joint in my body aches. Maybe I don't mind that Erik and I watch a lot of TV together, or that sometimes I spend days waiting for him to call, and that I've wondered what it would be like if he proposed. Maybe our life together *is* boring. But right now I miss being in a relationship with fewer…complications.

"What's wrong?" she asks, back in office attire and packing up her briefcase.

I shake off an answer and roll away from her, dried specks of blood still on my skin.

"After what you accomplished last night..." She sticks her bandaged hand in my face. "You should be very happy with yourself."

"We beat the shit out of each other and you lied to me about *everything*. Why should I be happy?"

She looks bewildered. "I think you're missing the point."

"I don't think I am." I painfully sit upright, barely able to hold the sheet covering me because my fingers are so swollen. "You told me you loved me and wanted us to be together."

"I do."

"Then tell me the truth about the videos, and the pictures, and the city inspector who never showed up last night, and why I found your ex-girlfriend Rachel locked away in an Iron Maiden!"

The cocky look on her face thaws. "I didn't lock her away." She slowly lowers herself next to me. "My uncle did."

I clasp the sheet tighter around my midriff. "How is that possible? You told me your uncle abandoned you."

She looks into my eyes, as though willing me to believe her. "I started escorting to make ends meet. A few years later, I showed up for a call and there he was." She bites at a fingernail. This time she doesn't stop herself from damaging her manicure. "He told me I was missing out on a better business model."

"Business model?" I absorb her words. "So all that about going to UCLA and taking photography was a lie too?"

"No," she says earnestly. "We started making enough money for me to go to college and I *did* want to pursue a real career. It's just..." She runs her hand slowly up my backside. "The money was so easy and the girls so plentiful, it was hard to stop."

Holy crap. I'm part of some prostitution ring. "And I'm just one of those girls."

Her head whips toward me. "Not even close." She curls a strand of my hair between her fingers. "You're the first person who's made me reconsider all this." Abruptly, she lets go and straightens. "But it's so complicated, Angie."

She smoothes out the creases in her skirt and walks into her dressing room. After a few minutes, she exits with a dress and tosses it at me.

I stare at the long black velvet number. My mouth gapes as I touch the familiar heart-shaped design. I want to ask her how she got the dress, but I know it's pointless. She has no reason to tell me her complicated truth anymore.

She leans over and a key pops out from under her blouse. Seeing that key tick-tock from side to side, regardless of whether it opens the front door, reminds me of how many times I've failed trying to outfight her in the week that we've been together.

"I thought you might want something special to wear. To celebrate our one-week anniversary." Pain creeps through her smile. She wishes it were a true celebration, but knows better. Now she's just reading some script she wrote a long time ago.

Her lips press against my forehead. "I'm going to make it a half-day today, so don't take too long getting ready."

I watch her leave, all bravado and grace. Her footsteps eventually disappear down the stairs.

My gaze shifts back to the Jessica Rabbit dress that up until this moment was hanging in Erik's closet. He loved it on me so much, he wanted me to be able to wear it whenever he demanded. I was overjoyed by the compliment. I knew I would probably only wear it for him anyway, on special occasions.

My hands run over the plush fabric in a dreamlike manner. I look at the tag inside. Lauren by Ralph Lauren. *That's my dress, all right.* And there's only one way she would have been able to bring it here. That's probably how she also got those pictures of me and Erik.

Panic sets in. I need to get a hold of him. He shouldn't have gotten tangled up in something I started. I need to make sure he's okay.

The charging unit for the stun gun is still on that countertop near the front door. I carefully slide off the bed, muscles stiff and sore. I look around for something to wear and spot my old tank top, jean skirt, bra, and underwear. They're cleaned and folded on the couch. *When did she find a chance to do that?*

There's no time to analyze.

Changing into the attire I showed up in feels odd. Everything is loose and the insecurities have faded.

My wedges are neatly lined up near that old chest she uses for a coffee table. I slip on the familiar footwear and limp back to the bed. I lift the mattress.

Luckily, my cell phone is still there.

I retrieve it and pace, trying to figure out where she would stash anything metallic.

She has those old food cans in that room with the Iron Maiden, but those aren't going to work. I need some kind of wire—

The wire in the darkroom.

It takes a few moments for my eyes to adjust to the faint red light when I walk in, but I notice she's been developing more pictures. I look closely.

More pictures of Rachel. I set my phone next to one of the bins so I can view the images better.

In this series, Rachel is stretched out on a cross in a leather harness that looks exactly like the one Heather had me wear on the whipping horse. There are clamps on her nipples and private parts.

At first she looks like she's enjoying herself. The come-hither look on her face can't be misinterpreted. But as I walk further down the row of pictures, I can tell that she's uncomfortable, even horrified, by what's happening to her. The last picture lies next to one of the developing bins. I pick it up. She's still tied to the cross, but the clamps stretch her painfully and she's bloodied. Long welts cover her body, like somebody has been hitting her with a belt. Her head hangs limp and I have this awful feeling that she's close to death. Maybe we all are.

Could all this have happened without my hearing a thing? I walk to the door at the back of the darkroom and twist the knob. Of course it's locked. I start shaking it, and then pounding on it, yelling out to see if anyone will answer me...but no one does.

Guilt engulfs me. I should have helped Rachel when I had the chance, even though she was delusional and I didn't have a plan. I shouldn't have been selfish and thinking only of my own survival.

Maybe there's still a way. If she's in that Iron Maiden, breathing, alive, maybe I can get to her in time. I'll tell her that I've figured out a way to charge my phone. She can tell me where the reception is best. We can work together to get out.

I yank at the wire the pictures are hanging from, but it's no use. It's bolted well on either side and there's no way she's left a screwdriver for me to use. It's too thick anyway, so I'd have to pry it apart somehow.

I drop to all fours and start crawling on the cold cement, hoping to find a scrap of something left behind on the floor or in a corner. That's when I spot it.

Next to some bottles of chemicals is a busted power outlet. The plate is off and the plug-ins have been yanked out. It looks like they broke and someone was trying to fix the contraption.

I start tugging on the wires. The thin cables dig into my skin and the drywall breaks away.

Finally I manage to get one loose and examine it. This should be enough.

I put everything back together close to how I found it, and then I grab my cell phone and get out of the darkroom. I know I can figure out how to make this work.

When I reach the charging unit, I think back to the industrial arts class I took in high school, even though my mother told me I was wasting my time. *In theory…*

I begin peeling back each wire from the bundle—one tiny strand at a time—and then twist together two small strands of copper at each end. I set one end of the wires against the exposed charger points of my cell phone and the other where the stun gun typically resides.

The charging light on my phone turns on.

My insides jump giddily. *My mother has been wrong about so many things.* I look at the clock on the wall. It's nearly ten a.m. I hold my hands as still as I can so the battery indicator can continue to add more bars while I think of a plan.

There's reception somewhere. I've seen Heather use a cell phone in here. I know having a fully charged battery will help me find it. *But then what?* Obviously I have to try to get a hold of Erik again and the police. Most importantly, I need to convince Rachel to work with me…if she's still alive. *Would Heather kill someone she once loved?*

The thought sickens me, but if Rachel's dead, maybe there's a way to use that to my advantage as well. Surely Heather doesn't want to be exposed as a murderer and spend the rest of her life behind bars.

An hour goes by and everything in my body is burning. My back from being hunched over, my arms from leaning on them, and my fingers from holding the wires and cell phone so precisely to the charging unit. I'm almost there, and I know she said she'd be home early today, but I have to try for full bars.

My muscles fatigue more with each passing minute, but after another twenty, the charge is complete. I drop the wires in relief and shake myself out like a dog coming in from the rain.

I turn on my phone, but it still says no service. I wander around, searching for that perfect spot, and end up at the wall of windows. I move the phone up one side, watching carefully to see if it's responding. I crank open some of the windows and hold the phone to the outside world, again hoping for that magical spot... until...service!

After a few moments, a flood of text messages populate my Inbox—all from Erik. Of course he's worried. I don't know why I ever doubted that. Even if he *did* fall into an indiscretion. Even if he *did* get in too deep with that website. I just hope he's okay. I start scrolling and scanning.

Call me back.

I'm sorry.

Are you safe?

Please call me back!

I'm really sorry.

Worried about you.

Are you mad?

Where are you?

Why haven't you been to any classes?!!?!

Do you know where you are?

I'm going to the cops.

My face lights up. He went to the cops.

If she broke in to get my dress and those pictures of us, he probably wasn't home. He was probably safe with the cops. They've probably been searching for me for days now and just need one last piece of information to find me here.

I look for any discerning landmarks, but Heather's loft is surrounded by tall nondescript walls that are crumbling apart. There's some faint writing on one of them.

It's at the very top and I can barely make it out, but eventually I discern that it says "Durango Corporation." It's probably a company that resided there a hundred years ago, but that might be a good enough clue.

I do my best not to move so I don't lose signal and quickly compose a text to Erik: *Help Me! Somewhere downtown. Old Durango Corp Building. Help!*

I hit Send.

A faint electronic beep resounds from inside the loft. It startles me.

I look around but don't see anyone.

The reception is still good on my phone.

I go to my contacts and when I reach Erik's name, I hit the Call button.

The phone starts to ring on my end.

A faint reciprocating tone rings from inside the loft.

My heart pounds in my chest as I walk towards the room that houses the Iron Maiden.

"Hello." A female voice answers the phone.

The signal starts to cut in and out as I grab onto a window ledge to steady myself. "Who is this?"

"This is Angie, Erik's girlfriend," the voice says with poise.

I take a deep breath and continue walking. "That's impossible, because *this* is Angie, Erik's...girlfriend." I put my hand on the doorknob. "Heather?" I twist the knob and swing the door open.

"Boo!"

I jump back, screaming, and drop my lifeline.

She stands in front of me with a Cheshire cat grin on her face. Her good hand holds a cell phone, and when she spins it between her fingers, I recognize the black industrial cell phone case with the worn fraternity "Are You a Leader?" sticker on the back. It's Erik's.

"Where is he?" I ask as calmly as possible, trying not to imagine the worst-case scenarios.

"I see Erik's girlfriend didn't bother dressing for the occasion, like I asked her to." She drops his phone and plants a heel into the screen. The crack of glass fills my ears. "I see you're more interested in running away with your boyfriend than breaking up with him." She grabs my arm and starts dragging me towards the Iron Maiden.

"Don't turn it around like that, Heather."

I struggle to free myself, but even with her one arm bandaged, she has a strength that's hard to compete with.

"You have no idea the sacrifices I've made for you, and was going to make for us, when all along you were the one lying."

She shoves me against the old shelving. A few boxes of crackers land on my feet.

"Just tell me that Erik's okay. He doesn't have to be a victim in this too."

She readies herself to open the large iron casket and I start whimpering. I have this awful feeling that when the door opens this time, a dead Rachel or my dead boyfriend will fall onto me.

"Just tell me you haven't hurt him!" I feel hysterical and helpless. I swing at her.

She stops my hand inches from her face.

"You want to know where your boyfriend is?"

The door of the Iron Maiden opens.

It's empty.

She shoves me inside and when I claw at her, she head-butts me. In a daze, I feel her strap me in. "Don't worry," she finally says when I'm in the same position I found Rachel in a few days ago, "I prefer more dramatic endings."

The door of the Iron Maiden shuts and I hear it lock.

"Enjoy the show," she says, her voice muted through the thick wooden chamber.

After a few moments of silence, a light comes on inside the Iron Maiden. It's a blue light from a small TV screen positioned in front of my face.

"I didn't want to have to show you this, Angie." Her voice floods the interior through speakers. "I thought you loved me."

The blue light on the monitor turns into a grey-toned video of an empty room. It looks like something shot with a security camera.

"I thought we had an understanding. Something special. I thought you respected yourself more than to be with someone who's cheating on you and being dishonest with you, but you continue to focus on *him*."

A woman steps into focus. She's tall and has long blonde hair. She's wearing a black bustier that cinches her waist and lifts her breasts, and a tight, short matching skirt. Her platform heels give the impression that she's even taller, but I know exactly who she is. She's the girl I thought was dead. The girl in all the pictures. The girl who didn't want to help me. The girl I wanted to try and save. The ex-girlfriend of the woman I thought I fell in love with.

Rachel is very obviously not dead. In fact, she looks like she's been fed well, taken a shower, and primped herself into a vixen.

She microwaves two mugs of water and then opens one of the tall cabinet doors in the kitchen area and takes out a plastic container. She scoops something into each cup and then retrieves a plastic pitcher from the fridge and tops off each mug with its contents. The scene is all too proverbial.

A knocking sounds, and Rachel grabs one of the mugs and struts over to a door that looks like the one I've been behind for a week now.

When she opens it, there's Erik. My head yanks forward. He treads in slowly, looking around, wearing his typical black t-shirt, jeans, flip-flops, and baseball hat with the lid turned backwards. "Cool place," he tells her, as she slides the door closed behind him and pulls on his arm towards a familiar leather couch.

They start to have a casual conversation, and she shoves the mug into his hands. He takes several long sips as he continues to look around. "Interesting art." He points to some portraits on the walls. They're of women captured in various erotic moments. She tells him that a good friend of hers took them and then asks if he's missed her. He chuckles awkwardly, like this isn't the first time they've met, and takes a few more long sips.

"I'm real worried about Angie," he says, placing the mug on the coffee table that looks like an old trunk, bouncing his knee like he does when he's restless. "You told me to come over. Let's start figuring this out."

"Some girls expect you to take a hint," Rachel replies. She leans in and starts kissing him, running her hands over him, not wasting any time. I'm already sick to my stomach, but the show goes on.

He grabs her like he wants to push her off, but then runs the back of his hand over the sweat that's formed on his brow. "Look, I barely remember what happened that night you showed up at the poker game."

Her hand cups his package and then unzips his jeans. "Let me remind you then."

He rubs his eyes and temples. She straddles him, and the skirt she's wearing slides up her bottom.

"I should just go to the cops—"

She covers his mouth and gyrates on him like a stripper.

Her hand slips into his jeans. His head rolls back and he mumbles something I can't decipher. I want to close my eyes. I want to scream at him to get out before it's too late, but something tells me it already is.

She shifts down and pulls his jeans lower, burying her head in his erection. He can barely lift his head upright. His hat tips back and his arms fold over his face as her blonde mane bobs up and down, over and over. "This isn't…this isn't what I expected." He struggles to talk.

She tells him she wants him inside of her and mounts him.

As I watch, I try to determine if his reactions are real or whether the coffee he drank has destroyed his plan to save me. But the noises he's making…

"Had enough yet?" Her voice swirls around the Iron Maiden and echoes in my brain. "Looks like your guy's a fan of all sorts of talent contests."

I stop myself from shedding any tears. I rationalize that she's only doing this because she wants to crush me. She knows I've gotten stronger and she's afraid I'm going to find a way to leave her for good.

The door of the Iron Maiden flings open.

It's Rachel. She's wearing the same outfit she was wearing in the video. Her lipstick is smeared, and she has a satisfied look on her face.

"You bitch!" I yell, thrashing violently against my bonds, the adrenaline pumping through my veins.

She puts her hands around my face. "You need to calm down, Angie."

Our eyes lock.

"Calm down, and I know I'll be able to get both of us out of here."

I stop struggling.

Erik's face swims in her eyes.

TWENTY-TWO

I'm standing in the middle of the loft where she's set up another stage. Everything is draped in black, live-theater style, and the chest that she's been using for a coffee table has been placed near one wall of curtains. The lights are so bright they ignite the stage, and everything else fades into pitch blackness except for the tiny red lights of video cameras. They're set to catch every angle of what I deduce to be her dramatic ending.

"At first I thought it was you." Heather's voice booms through the darkness. "That maybe you didn't have what it takes." She leads Rachel by the waist to where I'm standing. "But then you surprised me. Even more so than Rachel here."

She stops arm's length from me and pulls Rachel into her tighter. I notice she's wearing the holster with the stun gun slung over her right hip and protecting the hand that's still bandaged.

"Rachel here has been such a good girl, doing anything I ask her to. Doing anything *anyone* asks her to. Isn't that right, baby?" She dives in for a passionate kiss. Rachel responds, but I sense a misstep in their dance. Betrayal hangs thick in the air. I'm not the only one who's gotten hurt.

Heather walks over to the chest and leans down to open the latch. She pulls out two large daggers. "I know if I ask Rachel to kill you, she will."

If for a moment I doubted she would take things this far, I know now that the dangers have always been real.

She saunters back to where we're standing and places one of the daggers into Rachel's opened hand. Rachel smiles wide, as if she's been waiting to do this all along.

"Which brings me to you," she says, thrusting the other dagger against my chest. It lands heavily and almost slips from my fingers.

"I've come to the conclusion that your problem is you're not sure where your loyalties lie." She retrieves the key from around her neck. "And that's not good for business." She takes a few steps back and hangs the key around Rachel's neck. "Or pleasure."

Moments later, she's slithering behind me. The fingers of her good hand swim lightly across my shoulders and neck. Her lips brush against my ear. "I love you, Angie," she whispers, "but I'm ready to let you go."

The statement both crushes and relieves me. I almost don't want it to be true. As much as I hate her for hurting me in so many ways, I still love her too. I've experienced more emotional and sexual highs and lows with her in one week than I have in my entire life. And part of me doesn't want that to end. *What is normal supposed to look like after this?*

She turns my head and her mouth finds mine. "You get the key from Rachel, and you can walk right out the door," she says between kisses that are not telling the whole story. "I won't stop you this time. I promise."

I can see the rage in Rachel's eyes as she watches an intimacy between Heather and me that I know she doesn't have.

"Come *with* me," I plead quietly, my mouth more fervent. "It doesn't have to end like this." I'm hoping to reach beyond her status quo to that place I know exists but that she's afraid to tap into.

She stiffens and pulls away from me. She's made up her mind.

"If you can get the key, you can leave, Angie." She wraps her good hand around Rachel's torso. "But if I know Rachel..." She stops to nuzzle Rachel's head into her neck. "You're going to have to kill her first." She gives one of Rachel's breasts a sardonic squeeze. "Isn't she, baby?"

Rachel nods.

"If you're wondering..." Her gaze locks with mine as she plays with the key on Rachel's chest. "This key opens the door you need it to open."

The statement has cryptic overtones. I scramble to decipher what it could possibly mean as she picks up her camera and takes a seat in a director's chair.

"Whenever you're ready, ladies." She snaps a photo. "Do try to be dears," she adds, "and stay on the stage. We wouldn't want to disappoint anyone."

The clicks from her camera reverberate in my ears.

I grip my hands around the dagger.

Heather crosses her legs. The tight skirt she's wearing pulls on her thighs, and her calves flex, trying to locate a sturdy spot on the footrest for the platform of her heel.

As my toes grip at the leather lining of my wedges, I decide I'll be better served without them and kick them to the side. I can't believe she's making me fight to the death. We could've been long gone by now. All she had to do was open that door.

Unless there's someone else who wants to see more. The red lights of the video cameras blink in my periphery vision.

Heather leans forward, enough that her pillowy blouse exposes the mounds of her breasts secured in that black lace bra.

I should've killed *her* by now. I should've pounded a pillow over her sleeping head in the middle of the night, or spiked her drink with too much of something I found in her medicine cabinet, the way she did mine. Or bashed her head in with that bat when I had a chance. Even if I didn't have the right key, I would have figured out something.

I should have been brave enough. But in the end, my rage gave way to a greater emotion. Love. But also to the self-doubt I've been carrying all my life. Self-doubt brought about by years of conditioning. It was easier to go along unnoticed or yell "Bubblegum." We are all victims of circumstance—until we make a conscious decision not to be. I touch the blade with my fingers to gauge its sharpness.

Rachel's breathing becomes uneven and her nostrils flare. "I was always supposed to be her number one!" Dagger pointed forward, she lunges at me.

I don't react quickly enough and feel the blade nick my side. When I reach my fingers down and feel moisture, I realize her attack has damaged more than just my tank top.

She circles me, like a coyote closing in on its prey. "You think in a week you can take away what we've built over six years?"

Six years?!

She lunges again.

This time I hold out my dagger and catch her forearm with my blade. I can tell I've administered a pretty decent gash.

"I think after six years, she needs something different," I say, recovering. I start swinging wildly.

Something inside me is coming alive. I want her dead. Out of our life. I want to win this time.

Rachel lands a kick to my thigh and it throws me off balance. The dagger drops out of my hand and slides. I take a few steps towards it, but she grabs me in a headlock and we grapple.

Her dagger points at my throat, and I hold it off with everything I've got. She's taller than me, so I'm at a disadvantage. There's only one thing I can think to do. I kick back as hard as I can. The calloused skin of my foot feels her kneecap hyperextend. It cracks and turns to mush. She cries out in agony, but her grasp around my neck holds firm and we plummet to the floor together, landing on our sides. I start whacking her in the ribs with an elbow until I feel her weaken and am able to pry the dagger she's holding from her fingers.

I roll on top of her and hold the dagger with both hands above her chest. All I have to do is plunge it in…

"No, please don't!" she begs. "I-I'll just gi-give you the key." She offers me the metallic trinket secured around her neck.

She doesn't want to kill me. She just wants me to leave so she can have Heather all to herself again. Maybe that would be best for everyone.

My grip loosens for just a moment, but it's all Rachel needs. She grabs the dagger from my hands and butts my head with hers.

I tumble backwards, dizzy from the blow, and she follows me, stabbing at my upper body.

Feeling the tip at my shoulder, I'm able to twist away to prevent it from sinking past my outer layer of skin.

She hurls herself at me and I stick out my leg. My foot hits her diaphragm and she drops, wheezing for air.

I see my dagger and scramble towards it. As I pick it up and stand, my assailant sluggishly tries to get up on her one good knee. "I should...have...never...gone along...with the plan," she says between gasps of breath.

"What plan?!" I yell loud enough for everyone to hear, spinning round the room.

No one responds.

My attention shifts back to Rachel, still struggling to gain balance.

She had sex with your boyfriend, Angie. She lured him and seduced him. And now she wants to live happily ever after with the woman you love. What are you going to do to wipe that smug look off her face?

I let out a carnal cry as I leap at her. There's no time for her to plead with what's left of my compassionate side as I plunge my dagger into her neck, shredding through skin and tissues and arteries until I know it's over.

Rachel falls to the floor with a thud, and a pool of blood forms quickly.

I'm breathing hard and shaking, with more questions whose answers I'll probably never get. I rip the key from around Rachel's neck and extend my weapon.

Shutter sounds fill the room.

I turn to face Heather. She's still sitting in the director's chair. She lowers the camera, her face slack with astonishment. I can't tell if it's because she wanted me to win...or expected me to lose. But then I see her reach for the stun gun. She stands and walks towards me.

Shoving the key into the front pocket of my skirt, I shuffle away from her.

The key opens the door you need it to open. What does that mean?

I don't believe that after everything we've been through, that the key I ripped off Rachel's neck opens the front door of Heather's loft any more than the last one did.

I bolt for the darkroom, remembering there's another door in the back. I crank the knob to the darkroom, fling myself inside, and then slam my bodyweight against the door and turn the lock.

Heather bangs on it, demanding I let her in. I push the carts holding the development bins against the door as extra buffer. Then I look around. I see a light peeking through from the back wall.

I walk towards it.

I push on the door and it swings open.

TWENTY-THREE

The room is blinding white. The walls are stark and I can see my reflection in the sheen of the concrete floor. It's illuminated by a mixture of natural light from some windows and large, bright fluorescent lights that hang from the ceiling.

I slowly walk inside.

Two cubicles sit in the center, separated by glossy partitions, with one tall white wall behind them. It must be sixteen feet high, but it doesn't run the length of the room.

The cubicles are filled with the typical desk, chair, and computer equipment one would expect at a business office. Each has multiple monitors and they're turned on.

I sit down on a white leather office chair.

One monitor displays video editing software, and the frame is frozen on a close-up of my face. It's when she slicked my hair back in a bun, painted my lips red, and covered my eyes with that lace blindfold. My mouth is parted and I'm biting at my lower lip. I look like I'm at the height of ecstasy.

The next monitor has a browser open to a website. Stone Media, LLC. *For members only*, the window states, and then lists the options. My eyes blink rapidly as I read the familiar words. Monthly memberships start at ten thousand dollars and work up to the six-figure range. At the bottom of the page, the username and password boxes are already filled out. Trembling fingers click Enter.

She's right. There *have* been a lot of women and a few men. And we each have a profile...on *her* website. Mine is at the very top. The thumbnail is one of the first pictures she ever took of me. Right before the coffee kicked in. I click on it.

An all-too-familiar scene starts to play. It's the first time she made me dress up. I was the angel on all fours, beckoning to be tempered, and she was the devil wielding her riding crop. It's strange to watch myself spiral out of control. I've spent my entire life until now, composed and suppressing most ideas. But here I am, having an orgasm. I look vulnerable...yet powerful. As much at her mercy as she is at mine.

I close the window and pick another profile, and then another, watching the scenarios change from lovemaking to fucking to disciplining—just like the first time I came across this website. Except this time, there's no window popping up, trying to lure me to watch more. This time I'm logged in as Administrator. Every option is at my fingertips.

And then I land on it again. The clip that started this whole affair, and now answers every question I've had about what I'm doing here. The blonde and a brunette I've never met, yet they seem so familiar. Entangled in one another on a bed that could be any bed—except that now I recognize the thick bedposts, shackles, rings, and plethora of dark sheets. The lovemaking that very distinguishably bears the direction of the woman I've been making love to for a week now. Intense, demanding, purposeful. With an edge that most wouldn't dare cross.

I stop winding through the clip and close the window.

Now I'm part of it. People are watching *me* have what I consider the most mind-altering sex of my life. They're paying a lot of money for this privilege, but still…I didn't give her that permission.

A more chilling thought runs through my mind. I killed one of the girls on the website. Not the mastermind behind this crazy twenty-first-century version of prostitution, but someone who probably started out as innocently as me. And it was all recorded. *What has she done to me?*

My palms sweat and my eyes well with tears as I turn to the last monitor. It's divided into six security-style camera shots that loop through different rooms in what I presume is the entire space that's such a steal to rent. I catch a glimpse of one before it changes and immediately reach for the mouse so that I can bring it back. I click on a tab that says "previous image" and look down at a bird's eye view of a giant cross.

I've seen that cross before. In those pictures, with Rachel hanging from it. Except this time it's not Rachel. This time it's a man with dark hair and svelte muscles.

I hear someone cough, and the mouse veers out of my hand. I push off from the white desk and make my way further into the space. I grip onto the dagger hard as I peer around the tall white wall.

It's an almost identical loft. A gigantic bed sits in the middle, adorned with shackles and black sheets, another makeshift kitchen and more portraits on the walls with faces in the midst of rapture or pain…depending on what you've paid to see.

My eyes land on the large gothic cross I saw on the security screen. It's steadied on plywood at an angle…with Erik bound to it.

I want to scream, but my voice escapes me as I hurdle towards him.

His head hangs limp and his shirt is torn. "Oh my god." I move my dagger to my left hand and reach my fingers to feel for a pulse. He's alive.

I lift his head and touch his beautiful firm, tanned skin. "What did they do to you?" My fingers linger near a cut on his chest. The hair that always irritates him is starting to grow back.

I inch closer to his face. "So much has happened." I suddenly feel the need to explain myself. "Everything is so different."

I grab onto his black t-shirt. My cheeks are wet and my fingernails dig into him the way they did when we made love graduation night. "But I didn't want this to happen to us."

I think back to all the realizations I've had about myself in the time I've been here with Heather. Yet whenever I thought of escape, it was to be with him.

"Angie?" His voice is barely a whisper.

My fingers uncurl from around him and I shift back. "Yes, Erik, it's me."

I can tell he's trying to focus. "They drugged me." His head rolls to one side and his speech is slurred. "We need to get out of here before they come back."

I use my dagger to cut at the nylon chords. "I'm so sorry." I unwind the rope from around one of his wrists.

It drops and his face scrunches. "No, Angie, I'm sorry. This is all my fault."

I tell him it's not, and not to strain himself. But he tugs my chin to face him. "The night we were supposed to meet...this other girl showed up."

My heart sinks.

His hand grazes the fresh wound on my shoulder. "You're hurt." In more ways than he can imagine.

"How did you find this place?" I ask.

He inhales sharply. "She brought me here. She knew I was looking for you. She wanted to help. Told me not to go to the cops."

I start cutting away at the ropes around his pecs. "She, who's *she*?" Though I already know.

He tells me her name is Rachel. That she showed up at the poker game and really got the party started. Demanded they do shots. Wiped them all out of everything they'd brought. Then his phone died. He passed out on a couch and wasn't sure how he got home...but *she* was there when he woke up. When he couldn't get a hold of me, he returned her text messages.

I don't want to hear any more.

"We have to get out of here." The dagger gets through another rope...and then I hear the clicking of heels behind me.

"Well, well, the boyfriend and girlfriend finally reunited." Heather's voice fills the room and then is replaced by the revving of a drill. "Looks like I got here just in time."

I turn to point my dagger at her, but a heavy blow lands against my jaw. It knocks me back several feet and sends my dagger sliding several more.

"Get away from her!" I hear Erik rasp.

She holds up the cordless tool and puts a screwdriver bit into it. She tests the power again.

I get on my hands and knees and scamper towards the dagger.

"This can go one of two ways, Angie."

My hand clasps onto the dagger and I freeze.

"I can either drill this nail into his wrist, or his palm."

I look up at her and see her bandaged hand propping Erik's arm firmly to the cross. He's too weak to struggle free.

"If I go into his wrist, I think we both know the outcome and how quickly it will happen."

"What do you want, Heather?!"

She lifts the power drill again and manages to force his palm apart. "You, Angie. I just want you."

She puts the tip of the screw against his skin. "Except you're never really going to leave your boyfriend."

"That's not true!" I watch Erik writhe on the cross. "You had me. I was ready to leave my entire life for you."

Erik slumps his head in my direction, questions filling his eyes.

"That may true, but I'm never going to leave mine." She bores the screw through Erik's hand. He bellows, and I avert my eyes in horror.

"You're a coward!" I scream, as the electrifying sound of metal grinding through bone fills my ears. Blood bursts out from Erik's new wound and his head drops.

"Freeze! And put your hands up!"

My knuckles glow white as I turn towards the man who's burst into the room.

He's pointing a gun, and a police badge hangs from his neck. He could make anyone believe they'd just been rescued. Even the grey shirt under his dark suit looks official. Except I've seen him before…

Heather points the power drill at him. "Last time you knocked—Uncle Johnny."

He pauses at those words. As do I. He obviously hasn't heard them in a long time. Beads of sweat form at his brow and he runs a hand through his salt-and-pepper hair.

He looks from her to me. I stare back at the familiar square jaw and light green eyes. He's the city inspector—or at least that's the role he was playing that day he tore Heather and her loft apart.

"It's over, Heather," he says. "I'm putting an end to this right now."

She throws her head back and lets out a laugh. The drill drops from her hand with a loud thud and she raps her fingers on the stun gun at her hip. "Don't be ridiculous, Johnny."

She strides towards him, daring him to take her on.

Her cheek rubs against the barrel of his gun. "You always come back, like a bad cigarette habit." She rotates her head, moaning, lifting her skirt and grasping her thighs ecstatically.

"Not this time." He cocks the gun.

Her hands tighten around her crotch. "Oh, Johnny, you couldn't live with yourself knowing you could never be inside of me again, or feel my mouth on your cock." Her lips encircle the gun and she slowly bobs her head forward and back over the barrel.

I squint my eyes, barely able to watch. *Why isn't she using her stun gun now?*

His eyes grow red and wet and his breathing ragged as he slowly retracts his gun from her mouth. It drops to his side.

"That's what I thought," she says, sliding closer. She grabs his bulge firmly. "It's too hard to quit." She starts to unbutton his shirt.

He grabs her bandaged hand and squeezes. She gasps. He keeps crushing her hand until she's on her knees. When she whimpers, he grabs her by the throat and drags her across the floor, slamming her against a wall, pounding the gun next to her head.

He tears her blouse and pulls up her skirt. The buttons clink lightly as they land on the concrete floor.

"Please no, Uncle Johnny. Please, please, please, no," she yelps out like a little girl, with a twisted smile on her face, until he smothers her mouth with his and unzips his pants.

They're both incapable of stopping their ritualistic act.

I lift the dagger over my head and run at them, palms sweating, heart pounding in my chest. Each stride feels like I'm watching something in slow motion, where the inevitable is too many incremental moves away, until suddenly it's so close you want to press rewind.

I drive the dagger into his back.

He staggers, but manages to fire his gun.

The bullet hits Heather's leg, and she collapses.

He topples to the floor and convulses, mouth sputtering, eyes wide with shock.

I push him over with my foot and yank the dagger out of his back. I wipe the blood off and carefully stick it down the back of my skirt.

The gun is close. I pick it up.

Standing over him, I run my thumbs over the hammer. It's still cocked.

The year my mother left on that archeological dig with the other man, my dad took me to the firing range.

I had walked past his room one afternoon and seen him handling it. A .357 Magnum. I was scared, although I didn't know exactly why. I didn't even know he owned a gun. When he realized I was there, he told me to sit down on the bed beside him. He started telling me about the history of the weapon and teaching me the mechanics of shooting. The look of anguish eventually lifted off his face.

Later that day when we went to the range, I watched him wield that weapon with such precision. I wondered why my mother would ever want to leave a man like that.

I face my target square-on, feet shoulder-width apart, and lean slightly forward with bent knees. The way my dad taught me. I put both index fingers on the trigger and press back. The bullet fires into Johnny's back and the gun recoils. My ears ring and my shoulder blades hurt. Hot, dark blood spills out. I've killed him.

In a split second, I've changed everyone's fate.

My lip trembles as I rotate to face her. Her leg is hemorrhaging profusely, and I know what I *should* do. She's the last one left behind from the business that's been built up in this loft. I'm sure of it now. If I pull the trigger, Stone Media, LLC, will go away for good. No one else will ever end up a new profile.

"You killed him," she says, in a voice full of grief.

The weight of the barrel feels as heavy as my conscious. I know I've taken from her everything she was holding dear. And I did it… to give her a new start. With or without me.

"He wasn't good for you."

She slumps to the ground, reaching out one hand to grasp the concrete and pull herself forward. The bandaged hand is little help and her limp leg leaves a dark red streak as it drags behind.

She whimpers his name like a grieving widow and continues her journey until she reaches his ruptured torso and lies down next to him.

I toggle the safety lever back on and lower the gun, shuffling away from her and towards Erik, picking up the drill along the way.

"I heard a gunshot." He struggles to talk.

"I'm alright," I tell him, inspecting the screw deeply wedged in his palm. I tear my tank top, knowing the reverse experience is going to be just as traumatic.

"You need to hold on one more time," I prepare him.

I lift the power drill to his bloodied appendage and reverse the screw. He fights with everything he has to prevent from crying out. I quickly wrap his hand and go to work on setting him free.

It takes some time, but I eventually manage to cut and unwind all the rope and slide him off the cross.

I sling his arm over my shoulder as we stagger to the front door. Past a bed with dark sheets and ominous shackles, past a seductive leather couch, past a chest full of weapons and the couple who made this their home.

We reach a cool steel door locked with a deadbolt, again identical to Heather's. And this time I'm not confused. I reach inside the front pocket of my skirt and pull out the key I tore off Rachel's neck.

I stick it in the deadbolt and it clicks with ease.

Erik straightens with some renewed strength and helps me slide open the hefty exit.

A staircase just like the one I fell sick in a week ago waits on the other side.

We begin a slow descent out of the loft, careful not to further compromise the damage that's been done to both of us.

At the bottom of the stairs is an industrial grey door with a bar across it. I push it open to the outside world.

We're surrounded by remnants of downtown L.A., in a part that probably once supported a comprehensive rail network. An area that will be forgotten until developers decide to fill it with a new stadium and upscale housing. The low hum of cars making their way up and down the I-5 comforts my ears and the air over the valley emits a familiar light-brown haze.

I lean out and let my face bask in the sunlight for a moment. The warm rays and Erik's arm over me are a reminder of a time not too long ago where everything in my life was less…complex.

He pulls me closer. "I want to be with you, Angie." He rests his head against mine. "I thought you were mad at me, and then I was mad at you, but then I was so worried…I'm sorry I did some stupid things."

I push up on my tiptoes and press my lips against his cheek. "You weren't the only one."

He tugs on my tank and brushes his lips against mine. "I should never have gotten involved with Heather."

I lower my feet. "I thought you said her name was Rachel."

He grasps my hand. "I mean, it was…but there was this website. And Heather made it so easy to join." He coughs and winces. "She offered me a free trial. I think that's how they found *us*."

His eyes search mine looking for forgiveness—and affirmation that I still believe…

I step away from him, wriggling my hand loose. "You know how to get to a police station or hospital from here?"

"What are you talking about? Aren't you coming with me?" He holds out his hand, desperation in his voice. "I need you to come with me."

I shake my head, curling his fingers into a fist and kissing each knuckle before letting go.

My resolve stiffens…and he relents.

"When am I going to see you again?"

My fingers graze the stubble on his chest and the firm muscles of his pectorals. "I don't know."

I turn for the stairs.

"Angie, I love you!"

Erik has shouted the words I've wanted so long to hear, but I don't dare turn around.

I bound up the stairs before I change my mind.

TWENTY-FOUR

My stride shortens as I reach the last step to the door. I'm fully prepared for the worst. That she's dead, too, and I'm going to have to spend the next several months justifying my actions in the name of self-defense…and coping with my feelings.

Instead, I find her struggling with a pair of pliers wedged deep in her calf. A syringe, a small bottle of clear liquid, thick pads of gauze, and white vinegar lie near the leg that's been shot. Perspiration pours from her skin.

"I knew you'd come back."

I rest my hand on the gun wedged in my skirt, opposite the dagger. "Maybe just to watch you die."

"Because I'm revolting and you hate me."

"Love and hate are a lot alike. It's indifference that pulls people apart."

She smirks before attempting again to yank out the object lodged in her leg. "Wouldn't want to go through life setting off every metal detector."

"I think you've got more to worry about than metal detectors."

She looks around. "This place? Stone Media, LLC?" Laughing, she nods at the dead body still lying in the middle of the room.

"We've had years to cover our tracks and line the right pockets. Besides, there are too many members in this city with a lot more to lose than me."

"Erik's going to the police," I say, not believing she can possibly get away with all this.

"Johnny *is* the police, Angie. They're only going to investigate as far as one of Johnny's guys is going to allow them to investigate. Besides, as soon as they see Erik is a member, he'll be just as guilty as anyone else."

I step closer. Her face scrunches as her fingers slip from around the pliers.

I drop to the ground and take the rigid tool out of her hands. "You set him up."

Objection resonates in her face, but she knows she's not strong enough right now. "No. I was just going about my business."

She watches me flex the steel a few times and then carefully insert it into her gaping wound. "The people who join are always looking for something unusual. Stuff real fantasies are made of. Kink with a twist," she says in sing-song fashion. "And the girls I find are always looking for a walk on the wild side—and then money. They don't know or care what it does to me."

Her breathing becomes erratic as I grip the small piece of lead. "But then this girl logged in...as Erik. I knew it was a girl because the webcam was on. I watched her go through the clips and very purposely repeat one."

With one more heave I manage to yank it out.

She gasps.

We both stare at the dark red debris clamped between the pliers.

"I could tell she was looking for something...different." Her eyes soften. "It stirred something in me."

I let everything drop with a thud and reach for the vinegar. I splash it over her gushing wound.

She's smiling. "Except she didn't log in again. Just the real Erik. I suspected that if I got Erik, I'd find the girl again. And I did."

I reach for the gauze and press it down. "You had a plan for me from the beginning."

The white pads turn red. "I had a feeling about you."

"Then why put me through all this? We could've had some fun, you could've fulfilled some of your clients' needs, and then we could've left or you could've let me go. No one had to die." I thought a minute. "Or does everyone end up like Rachel?"

"I don't have as much blood on my hands as you think." Heather pinches her thumb to her index finger, rubbing the red color between them. "But me and Rachel, we were too entangled in all this with Johnny. I needed to keep up appearances, and test you. Make sure you were strong enough to set both of us free."

I spot a video camera on a tripod to my right *and* left. In fact, I see four red lights blinking all around the space. *She's been recording it all.* This is just another chapter in a series that someone's paying a lot of money to watch. Next to one of the video cameras is a photo camera.

I place her hand over the gauze, making sure she's applying adequate pressure. I walk over and twist the camera off its stand.

"You were good," I say facing her, playing with the lens.

I kneel down next to her again and wipe the hair and blood from her face. She's shaking a bit and her breathing is shallow. I snap a photo. "Stay with me."

Her mouth curls into a faint smile.

I continue snapping pictures.

TWENTY-FIVE

I walk past the roped-off line and greet the big black bouncer. I lean slightly so he can peek at the cleavage popping out of my cowl-neck top. He takes a moment to check out the way my tight leather shorts hug my behind. I give him a lingering peck on the cheek to tantalize a possibility that doesn't really exist.

He lifts the rope to let me in.

I strut down the narrow hallway in my tall platform heels and watch a couple grope and kiss and fall against the wall. The girl grabs on to the bottom of the guy's shirt and tugs hard, hiking up one leg around him. His smooth muscles bulge every time he moves. It reminds me of a time long gone now...

I step into a large two-story space. The club is packed, and everyone looks high on life. The dance floor is saturated with leggy women. Off to the side, men look longingly at them.

I make my way through bodies that undulate in their small square footage of allotted space. Sometimes they swell smoothly, other times they calibrate fiercely, but the DJs tantric beat never lets up. I nuzzle up to a pair who look open to suggestions.

She wears a short black bob with wispy bangs that accentuate her soft Filipino features, and her animal-print dress drapes her body in a flattering way. He's some kind of African-Latin mix, which gives his face an exotic flair and his body, clad in tight jeans and a fitted polo shirt, a rippling presence. It's the exact type of couple you would expect to find on the dance floor in a bustling metropolis like L.A.

I gyrate to their rhythm, my chest pressing into his back, every now and then brushing his side, until he pulls me between them.

She wedges her thighs between mine and grips my hips. I lift my arms and wrap them behind my head around his sturdy neck, leaning back against his firm abs. His crotch grinds against me as her hands run up my top. Her pouty mouth inches closer to mine.

I know it's what her boyfriend wants, but I tug her hair back, teasing, and turn my gaze towards the bar.

Through the veil of smoke and rainbow of lights, I see her. You couldn't miss her if you tried. Those long legs that stiletto heels were built for, leading up to a perfect heart-shaped behind.

She's looking at me in the mirrored wall behind the bottles of booze, and when I catch her, she smiles and brings her beer up to her lips.

I excuse myself from between the couple and walk over to her.

When I arrive, she pushes her bottle towards the bartender, signaling it's finished, and picks up her clutch. I notice the scar on her right hand is almost gone.

"Leaving so soon?" I ask, resting a tall heel on the bottom rail of the bar.

She tosses her hair to one side. "I was waiting for someone. But I don't think they're going to make it tonight."

A breeze of cool air flows out of the vent right above us and I catch a whiff of her Chanel No. 5. "Well, I'm *someone*." I hold out my hand. "Angie."

"Heather," she responds, shaking it firmly.

"Can I buy you a drink, Heather?" I ask, already waving down the bartender.

He eagerly strolls in front of us. I tell him to get me another, and her a beer.

We smile at one another. Like two people who know each other intimately.

It's hard to let go of the ones we truly love.

Photo: Raphael Rogers

S.L. Hannah was born in Poland, grew up in Canada, and moved to Southern California to pursue her love of single-engine airplanes. *The Need* is her first erotic thriller. Visit her online at **www.slhannah.com** to learn about her work under other pen names, to get updates about her next book, and to connect through social media. S.L. Hannah lives in Los Angeles, California, with her husband. When she's not writing fiction, she continues to solve the aviation problems of the world.

LETTER FROM THE AUTHOR

Dear Reader,

First of all, thank you! Writing a book is an incredibly emotional journey. And after all the research and editing followed by feedback from beta readers followed by more editing, it is a thrill to finally be able to share this story with you. But the journey doesn't end once a book is published. It is truly another beginning.

As an author, your greatest hope is for the journey to continue, as the story lingers in the minds and hearts of your readers. You seek to inspire their own soul-searching as well as conversations about your book with their friends, and friends of friends.

You can help me keep that dialogue going by reviewing this book online, on Amazon, Goodreads, Kobo, iBookstore, All Romance Ebooks, Barnes & Noble, and/or Shelfari. Your words and ratings on those platforms really do make a difference and help me stay writing as an author.

I know *The Need* is a wild and thought-provoking story—one I never thought I would write. But after reading my husband's screenplay, I couldn't stop thinking and talking about it with my friends and colleagues. On the next page, I've compiled a list of some of our questions and discussions for you to consider in your own circles and book clubs.

Thank you so much for your support in continuing this intriguing conversation.

xoxoxox,
Hannah

READER DISCUSSION QUESTIONS

1. Is Heather really a bad person, or a psychopath, or did she get tangled in a wicked web?
2. Were Heather's machinations all a setup for Angie to become ensnared in Stone Media, LLC or for Heather to finally escape?
3. Did Angie really love Erik or was she looking to leave her relationship all along?
4. Did you find yourself rooting for Angie to end up with Heather or to leave with Erik?
5. When Uncle Johnny bursts in at the end, does he really intend to turn over a new leaf or is it just another part of his and Heather's sordid ritual?
6. Was Heather's relationship with Rachel real, or did Heather just use Rachel as another card in her game of luring strangers to her loft?
7. Was Erik completely innocent or did he get in too deep with Heather?
8. How did Angie's childhood relationship with Janelle shape her adult views of relationships?
9. Does our on-demand, social-media-focused world promote idealistic views of relationships?
10. Is the lack of privacy on the Internet and through social media promoting voyeurism and stalking?
11. Has our sexuality become more open or more repressed because of the Internet?
12. Is a rampant consumerism culture the real culprit behind thinking that we can buy and sell even the most precious and private of experiences, like sex?
13. How do our associations with words like "slut" or "whore" impact women's sexuality?

14. Is Angie gay, subconsciously in the closet all along, or is attraction based on our individual experiences with the people we meet?
15. Did Heather really intend for Angie vs. Rachel to be her final video, or was it just another episode in the continuing broadcast by Stone Media, LLC?
16. Do Heather and Angie have a shot as a "normal" couple in the real world or will they continue the status quo...and Stone Media, LLC?

What do you think?

Let me know by connecting with me on Goodreads and starting a discussion: https://www.goodreads.com/sl_hannah

CONNECT WITH ME

If you are interested in reading my future books, please sign up for my newsletter and exclusive offers at: www.slhannah.com. I can assure you that my next erotic thriller, *Open Endings*, will be just as provocative.

You may also be interested in my alternate-genre publications, including my acclaimed chick-lit series, *Sex, Life, and Hannah*, and my foray into a dark fairytale world with the award-winning *The Dentist and the Toothfairy*.

On the Internet:

www.slhannah.com
www.goodreads.com/sl_hannah
www.facebook.com/sexlifeandhannah
www.twitter.com/sexlifehannah
www.instagram/sexlifehannah

Other book websites:

www.sexlifeandhannah.com
www.thedentistandthetoothfairy.com